THE
POTTER'S WHEEL

THE
POTTER'S WHEEL

NORMA JOHNSTON

MORROW JUNIOR BOOKS
NEW YORK

The publisher and author gratefully acknowledge permission to reprint lyrics from "Turn! Turn! Turn! (To Everything There Is a Season)," words from the Book of Ecclesiastes, adaptation and music by Pete Seeger; TRO—Copyright © 1962 Melody Trails, Inc., New York, N.Y. Used by permission.

Library of Congress Cataloging-in-Publication Data
Johnston, Norma.
The potter's wheel.
Summary: When sixteen-year-old Laura attends her
wealthy, strong-willed grandmother's birthday
celebrations in a village in Pennsylvania her
grandmother is restoring, she becomes dramatically
reacquainted with various relatives, hears of the
dissolution of her parents' marriage, finds out some
of her own strengths and talents, and learns what
makes her grandmother interfere so forcefully in the
lives of her family.
[1. Grandmothers—Fiction.   2. Family life—Fiction.
3. Self-realization—Fiction]   I. Title.
PZ7.J6453Po 1988   [Fic]   87-24697
ISBN 0-688-06463-9

For Frank and Virginia Patterson—
love and shalom

THE
POTTER'S WHEEL

I

Aunt Lisa's portrait of me hangs over our living room mantel in Elm Grove, Wisconsin. It was her present to me on my tenth birthday, and I can still remember every moment of it, sharp and bright. I remember the crackle of the tissue paper as I tore it off, and the warm laughter in Aunt Lisa's voice.

"Portrait of a Young Van Zandt," *Aunt Lisa said to Mother,* "second edition, that is. Remember, Kay?"

Kay is my mother, and her *mother painted* her *at the same age and called it by that same name. It's a pretty good painting, though not as good as Aunt Kay's work, of course, but Mom has it stashed away in the guest room. She says that's because that's where Gran stays when she comes to visit.*

"Don't you mean Portrait of Laura?*" Mother answered Aunt Lisa tartly. "In point of fact, not one of us is a Van*

1

Zandt. Neither is Mother, since her marriage—a little item she seems to have forgotten." Whether she'd been referring to Gran's name or marriage she had not spelled out, and the comment had gone over my ten-year-old head. Now that I'm sixteen and a half, I wonder sometimes.

In point of fact (one of Mother's favorite expressions), it had been darn diplomatic of Aunt Lisa not to name the painting Portrait of Serena's Granddaughter, *because every time I look at it I'm struck by the resemblance between it and photographs of Gran when she was young.*

I wish I could talk to Mother about that, among other things. Mom's great to talk to, so long as it's not about the family. I know why. It's because she grew up hating being known as "Serena's daughter." With the implication, to outsiders anyway, of "How come this kid's so different?" That can still rankle, even when the difference is by deliberate choice.

Mom says her philosophy is, if you've got a charismatic parent, you've got three choices—compete and run the risk of being a poor copy; give up and get swallowed; or cut loose and be your own woman.

Dad says, not in Mom's hearing, "The trouble is, Kay sees herself as galloping off to create a brave new world, but she's still got a mother complex like a burr beneath her saddle, and she's never accepted the fact that beneath the wisecracks and the let-it-all-hang-out and to-hell-with-glamour, she's being exactly like Serena in her very different way."

I'm not sure which gets to Mother most, the Van Zandt

glamour or the Van Zandt celebrity. Not just Gran's—there's Aunt Lisa's deserved reputation as a painter. Not to mention Aunt Rena's reputation, which I'd rather not get into, or my cousin Sophie, who's apt to be either notorious or dead before she's twenty. And then there's Great-Aunt Alexandra, whom I've never met except in the society pages of slick magazines that resurrect her every now and then.

I give Mother credit—she's no hypocrite. She actually used a fake name to get her first job as a cub reporter, and she won't touch a penny of the trust fund set up when Great Grandpa Van Zandt struck it rich. She's always been strictly Kay Harris Blair, reporter; Mrs. Kenneth Blair, architect's wife; Laura Blair's mother.

"Lucky you," Mom said to me ruefully last year, when an article she submitted to The New York Times Magazine *got turned down. "You don't know what it's like to have a famous parent." And I nobly refrained from telling her how I used to feel when she was writing that "Super-mom" column for a Milwaukee paper. I was eleven, and the paper ran a small photo of her (awful, like a mug shot) at the top of the column, so mothers of kids I knew in school used to recognize her in the supermarket and burble out their problems, and I* died.

I lived through it. I'll live through whatever comes this summer. I am, after all, Serena's granddaughter, and the Van Zandts are survivors.

At least Aunt Lisa didn't name that painting Portrait of Serena Number Six.

"Over my dead body," Mother says often, blowing the

wisp of a brown curl out of her eyes, "would I ever inflict a number *on a child of mine! Thank God Rena's my mother's oldest child—she got stuck with carrying on the family name." Then she giggles and adds, "Look what she's done with it! I'll bet Grandpop and Grandmama are turning over in their graves!"*

Mother couldn't do anything about the aquamarine eyes and mahogany-colored hair I inherited from Gran, but she's done her darnedest to prevent any nongenetic Van Zandt tendencies and is probably relieved that I'm more shy than charismatic. She named me Laura because nobody in either family has the name, but she lost the battle with Dad when it came to my middle name. I'm Laura Serena Blair. Dad happens to like Gran, and that tells you a lot about my father.

Aunt Lisa gave that portrait, which had won a big prize at a British exhibition, to me, age ten. That tells you a lot about Aunt Lisa's understanding of kids, and of why she's my favorite aunt. And Mom hung the portrait over the living room mantel. That tells you a lot about how much Mom and I love each other. In spite of everything.

❦

It was one of those moments I'd always remember, sharp and bright. Early June, late afternoon. Dad was still at work, and Mother was out mailing a manuscript when the telephone rang. When I answered, a crisp voice said in my ear, "Western Union. Telegram for Katherine Harris Blair from Denver, Colorado."

All I could think was that something had happened to Gran. *"Wait a minute!"* I shouted, diving frantically for something to write on. By the time I had a ballpoint pen and an old envelope and had mumbled breathlessly, "Okay, go ahead," I was imagining the worst.

When I had the message down, I stared at it dumbly:

KAY DEAR NO REPLY TO EITHER OF MY LETTERS VERY ANXIOUS PLEASE CABLE YOU WILL ALL COME TO VREDEZUCHT MIDSUMMER'S EVE PLEASE DEAR DO NOT FAIL ME IT MEANS MUCH LOVE TO ALL KAY DARLING MOTHER

Vredezucht . . . that was the name of the Van Zandt home village that Gran's been restoring in Pennsylvania. Vredezucht means "breath of peace" in Dutch. Not exactly an appropriate name, considering the sparks that shoot in Mother's eyes whenever she hears Gran's project mentioned. Gran couldn't help but know that, I thought blankly. So why is she inviting Mother—no, *us*—out there now?

At that moment my father wandered in from work. I held out the message. Dad looked at it and whistled.

"I thought your mother was a bit more frenetic than usual the past couple of weeks. This explains it."

"Explains what?"

"Explains why she's been as un-pin-down-able as mercury. Your grandmother must have invited us for her birthday, and your mother doesn't want to go." Dad went to the roll-top desk and started rummaging. "I wonder what Serena's cooked up? Her invitation must be around here somewhere."

That was when Mom walked in. Her hair was ruffled and her face was flushed, and she looked very pretty in a slapdash, autumn-leaf sort of way. She also looked mad, which was explained by the Express Mail package she was holding. She must have gotten to the post office too late to mail it. Mother looked at my dazed face and then at Dad, who was rooting around, and demanded, "Would you two mind telling me what you're looking for in my private drawers?"

"An invitation that apparently came for all of us," Dad said calmly. "Your mother just telegraphed. Wants to know why she hasn't heard whether we're going to Pennsylvania. Excuse me for asking, Kay, but going to Pennsylvania for what?"

"What difference does it make?" Mother asked, too brightly. "You couldn't take the time off. You never can take the time off anymore. And even if you could, no way would I traipse back to Pennsylvania just because the Queen has sent a summons!" *The Queen* is what Mother calls Gran when she's really feeling ticked off at her.

"Now, Kay," Dad said reasonably. Dad has been responding to Mom's outbursts with "Now, Kay" for as long as I can remember, and it always makes her climb the walls.

"Don't 'Now, Kay' me," she retorted. "Laura and I have been trying to get you to take a vacation for three years, and your answer's always the same. You can't spare the time."

I hated it when Mom said, "Laura and I," like that, using me as an ally against Dad. I didn't say so; I never said it; anyway, you can't argue with Mom when she's wound up. All you can do, as Dad once said, is sit back and enjoy the fun. It is fun, provided you're not part of it.

Dad caught my eye, and when Mom wasn't looking he winked at me. I winked back, and the tightness in my stomach eased.

Mom was working up one of her better heads of steam. "How many times in the past three years have you said, 'Now, Kay, as soon as I can get a few weeks free, we'll go to England!' *England*, Ken, not Pennsylvania. Laura's sixteen; it's time she had her horizons broadened, and you know you've been promising me England so I could do that research on the effect of the Common Market on the British class structure!"

I've long since given up trying to figure out where Mom gets her ideas for subject matter—maybe it's the Van Zandt originality kicking up in her after all, a possibility I have more sense than to suggest aloud.

What I did do at that point was start to giggle, right in the middle of Mother's eloquence. This had the happy result of stopping Mother's monologue dead, as both my parents stared at me in surprise.

"I'm sorry," I said sheepishly. "You mentioned England, and that made me think of Sophie. If Gran sent invitations to the whole family, can't you imagine what's going on between Sophie and Aunt Rena right now? Sophie's still hooked on that rock star, isn't she? What do you bet she'll show up with him in tow?"

After a startled minute, Mother's indignation dissolved in giggles. "That," she said, "is almost worth going to the party to see. Not that I will."

"At least," Dad said with a twinkle, "let's see the invitation. Just so Laura and I know what we're missing."

Mother finally found it. Gran wasn't just having a birthday party. She was throwing a major extravaganza, running through an Old-Fashioned Independence Day with a dedication of the restored family homestead.

Dad got a faraway look in his eyes. "We wouldn't have to stay for the entire month Serena asks for. I couldn't get off that long, anyway. But just for the week of Serena's doings—come on, Kay! I'll try to arrange some time off in September and we can go to England then."

Mother's face was a study of conflict. "Laura will have school then," she said reluctantly.

"So we go without her, just the two of us. I can stand that if you can," Dad said blandly. "Laura can get her horizons widened at your mother's, particularly if Rena and Sophie show up." Deadpan, he copied

Mother's trick of waiting two counts and then delivering the whammy. "Of course, if you can't go to the party as a matter of principle, Laura and I can go without you. And can explain the situation to your mother. Or Laura could go alone."

"Over my dead body," Mother exclaimed in ringing tones, "will a daughter of mine set foot in Serena's fantasyland without me there to see she does not get hooked!" She stopped dead, her mouth still open. Then, to my infinite relief, she burst into laughter and threw her arms around my father. "Ken Blair, you are a devil!"

"That's what a gorgeous brunette used to tell me," Dad said complacently. "Journalist, I think she was. Picked her up on the Syracuse University campus, as I recall."

"Don't call me gorgeous," Mother said firmly. " 'Brilliant,' if you like. 'Genius' would also be acceptable. And I recall, *I* was the one who did the picking up. Not that it matters!" She swept my father into another extravagant hug.

So Mother telegraphed Gran our acceptance of the invitation, and the discussion ended on an up note. But the undercurrents lingered. And then suddenly they weren't just undercurrents anymore.

It was another indelible moment I'd remember without benefit of writing it in my journal. Mom's always pushing journal writing on me, because she keeps hoping I'll follow in her footsteps as a reporter. I don't know what she thinks that would prove. The last time I kept a diary was when I was eleven and had a crush on the kid who sat behind me in History. He and his pals found the diary while they were at my house for a Halloween party. The journal Mother gave me, hopefully, last Christmas has nothing in it but homework assignments and scrawls to remind me where I'm going and what I'm doing and who with; it's more like a calendar than a diary. And here and there are cryptic notes about rumors, or who's making out or breaking up with whom. It had nothing about my feelings in it, and I did not write about that family fight. I wanted to forget it, not remember it.

Dad got home late that night, on account of making a presentation to a client, and Mom got home even later. I remember she was in a really great mood, so great that she tossed me her car keys and said, "Laura, would you feel inclined to drive over to Sal's and pick up a pizza or two? With all the trimmings!"

Never one to refuse a chance to take the car, I made for the door.

Forty minutes later, bearing one sausage and mushroom and one Sal's Gargantua Special (anchovies extra), I walked into the worst confrontation my parents have ever had. That's what Mother calls them, *confrontations,* and she thinks they're healthy. I don't know what Dad calls them, but I know his face was very white and he was getting quieter and quieter, which is a bad sign because it makes Mother get even louder.

Mother hadn't just been at the newspaper office in Milwaukee, or out covering a story. She'd been having lunch with an editor-at-large from a national magazine. I should explain that Mom's what she grandly calls a "free-lance journalist," which means she sells articles to the local papers and, when she can, to magazines. Mostly she spends a lot of time doing "deep background" for articles she doesn't get around to writing. But she had written an article, a good one, on changing lifestyles in Britain, after Aunt Rena's latest visit. Aunt Rena had cried on Mother's shoulder about her own latest romance, and Sophie's rock star, and the cost of living in London, and so on; and Mom had written a feature story (not including Aunt Rena and Sophie, of course) which had run in a Chicago magazine.

And now a much bigger magazine wanted to commission Mother to write an in-depth story on the subject and was willing to pick up the tab for research expenses. Mother wanted to leave for England right away.

I knew what was going to happen, and it did. Mom sent Gran another telegram, saying we couldn't come. Mom packed her suitcase (one-third clothes, her favorite kind that Aunt Lisa calls "Kay's thrift-shop journalist chic"; two-thirds portable office-survival kit). Mom got wound up in a typical Kay Blair spin, talking faster and faster, filling me with lots of good advice and wishing me well on my final exams. Dad got quieter and quieter. And Mom left for England.

The same night that Mom left, on a night plane to New York so she could see the magazine editor there before catching her plane for London, our phone rang at two-thirty in the morning. There's a phone by my bed, and I grabbed it on the first ring. "Person-to-person call from London for Miss Laura Blair."

"Uh-huh," I said, struggling up from sleep.

Immediately, an excited voice overrode the operator's spiel. "Laura? Oh, great, I didn't want to get Aunt Kay! Look, has Mummy called you guys? Because if she has—"

"*Sophie?*" I sat up, suddenly wide awake. "Do you know it's two-thirty a.m. here? What's the matter?"

"Sorry," Sophie said unrepentantly. "It's seven-thirty here. Not quite my hour either, but I just got in."

"What are you doing in London? I thought you were in school in Switzerland!"

"I ran off. Laura, just shut up and listen. I'm in the public call box in Leicester Square, and I haven't got much change. Mummy and I had a row because she's insisting on dragging me to Gran's dreary old party, and you know how the family freaks me out!" Nothing near to how Sophie freaks the family out, I thought, grinning to myself. Sophie was rushing on. "So I cut out yesterday before Mummy showed up to collect me. She hasn't phoned Aunt Kay yet, has she?"

"No, she hasn't."

Sophie gave a sigh of relief. "She will! Now, what

I want is for you to convince Aunt Kay that I'm all right, so she'll convince my mum."

"*Are* you okay?" I asked apprehensively. Sophie giggled.

"I am now. Don't be such a prude, Laura, I'm not stoned! What I wanted was to hang out with this real cool musician I've been seeing—he's in London, that's why I came here; only he wasn't interested, so here I was, out on my bum in the middle of the night—"

"Deposit five pounds fifty or your call will be disconnected," the operator interrupted.

"*Reverse the charges!*" I shouted. "Sophie? What are you going to do?"

Sophie giggled again. "Not to worry! I hunted up Jay Tremaine."

"Who?"

"You know, Great-Aunt Alexandra's great-grandson! I knew he lived here, but I haven't seen him since we were in nursery school." Now that we were paying for the phone call, Sophie was in no hurry. "He is a definite hunk. On the scale of one to ten, I'd say a twelve. Guess what? He's invited to the command performance, too. So if Mummy calls, have Aunt Kay convince her that I'm fine and that I'll show up in Pennsylvania like a good girl, escorted by our cousin. Thanks a heap, Laura, you're a pal."

"Don't hang up!" I said quickly. "Sophie, Mom's on her way to London. She's going to be staying in a bed-and-breakfast place somebody recommended near Sloane Square." I scrambled frantically for the address and Mother's arrival time. "Go talk to her, Sophie, please!"

"Maybe I will at that. Ta for now."

The line went dead.

I hung up, too. Dad came into my room at this point, wondering if the call had been from Mom. I filled him in, and he grimaced. "I hope Sophie does go talk to Kay. She's at her absolute best dealing with this particular kind of family mess."

Dad was right. Mom's and Sophie's personalities, oddly enough, meshed better than either of them did with the rest of us. "Speaking of messes," I said, "what about Aunt Rena? Do we call her?"

"Let's cross that bridge when we come to it," Dad said. "Probably your mother will get to her in time."

Before she could, Aunt Rena called us. Dad and I calmed her down. Aunt Rena was extravagantly relieved to hear that Mother was on her way to London where, in her words, Mom could "talk some sense into my impossible child! I'm sure *I* can't! I'm the last person Sophie listens to these days!"

"Some wonder," I said, as Dad put down the phone.

"Some child." Dad's eyes grew reminiscent. "I wonder what color Sophie's hair is these days?"

The next thing that happened, other than exams and Dad's car breaking down, was my getting a letter from

Aunt Lisa's daughter Beth. She's two years younger than me, is going to be a dancer, and is shy. Her letter troubled me, though I couldn't be sure exactly why. We like each other, but don't see each other often, and her letters never tell me much of what's going on inside. This time, there was an uncharacteristic line: *I hope you're going to be at Gran's birthday party. I hope we get a chance to talk. I wish we lived closer to each other.* The paper looked as if she'd written something more and then erased it.

That was Monday. On Tuesday was my last exam. I went home after it, feeling oddly deflated, wishing I wasn't returning to an empty house. Only it wasn't empty. Dad was there, holding the telephone in one hand and packing his carry-on suitcase with the other.

I blinked. "Are you going somewhere?"

"To Philadelphia. There's another emergency at that shopping center site. I have to leave in an hour, and I can't get Mrs. Jensen on the phone."

Mrs. Jensen was the lady next door. "I can stay here alone, for heaven's sake," I said, reading his mind.

"Your mother would kill me." Dad paused, and a gleam came in his eye. He put down the receiver. "You don't have anything important in school from now on, do you?"

"There's only a day and a half left, and they're just putting in time so the school gets its federal funds."

"Good. You're coming with me," Dad said promptly.

"We'll have to take the Chevy; my car's still not fixed. How soon can you be packed?"

"As fast as you can. What should I take?" My heart lifted.

"Oh . . . a variety of things. Enough for a week or so, in any situation. You know," Dad said ambiguously.

We took off in the late light of evening. It was almost the longest day of the year now—Midsummer's Eve, Gran's birthday. I was very quiet as Dad pointed the old Chevy toward Pennsylvania, and he looked across at me and smiled.

"Wishing you were going to Vredezucht instead of Philadelphia?"

"Kind of."

Mostly we rode in silence, but it was a comfortable silence. Dad's mostly laid-back, though when he puts his foot down it stays put. He's good company, in a subtle sort of way. I'd almost forgotten that, I thought, surprised. Mom's such a whirlwind that when she's around it's hard to be aware of anyone else, even though she and Dad and I are a tight family unit and always spend a lot of time together.

Correction: *used* to spend a lot of time together.

We stopped for dinner outside Chicago and then started driving again. It was nice being on the road at night, and since traffic was light Dad let me take the wheel. We finally stopped for the night at a motel somewhere in Ohio.

We started out again soon after dawn. "Curl up in the back seat and get some more sleep," Dad said.

"I want to drive some more," I protested.

"You will, I promise."

He let me take the wheel after lunch. We were entering Pennsylvania now. A sign said PITTSBURGH–PHILADELPHIA–NEW YORK. And then, in less than an hour, PITTSBURGH AIRPORT NEXT LEFT.

"Turn off here," Dad said. I goggled. "Turn off," he repeated, smiling. "You're going to drop me off to catch a plane for Philadelphia, and then you're going to take the car on to Vredezucht. I mapped the route all out for you last night after you fell asleep. You'll only have to be on the highway for another hour, and anyway I'm proud of the way you handle the car. Just promise you'll phone me in Philadelphia tonight, to let me know you arrived all right."

That's another thing I'm always going to remember, the fact that Dad made it possible for me to go to Vredezucht.

I was thinking of that after I dropped him off and started, very carefully, back on the Interstate. Of that and of the ten fits Mom would have when she found out.

And of another thing I didn't want to think about at all, a thing that brought a fluttering of fear inside me in spite of my stern resolve.

After a while, I started thinking about Gran, and Sophie, and Beth's letter. The flutter of fear was replaced by the half apprehension, half excitement of anticipation.

My hands tightened on the steering wheel. I rolled the driver's window all the way down, and the country smells and sounds flooded over me.

Don't get your hopes up too high, kiddo, I could almost hear Mother's voice saying at my shoulder. Not cynically, but with a kind of rueful protectiveness.

A small white sign loomed: WELCOME TO VREDE-ZUCHT.

Breath of peace. The name lodged like the scent of dried rose petals in the atmosphere. It was like the ghost of a yearning I'd had as long as I could consciously remember, had never confided to anyone, not even to my parents. A yearning for a circle to call my own, a circle of peace.

Maybe, just maybe, going to this family reunion would provide it. Because Vredezucht *was* Van Zandt home turf.

But peace was a matter not just of place, but of people. And it was this fact that caused the butterflies to flutter more violently in my midsection as I carefully turned left, following the neat arrow in the sign.

How terrible if I should have come to Vredezucht only to discover that the peace it seemed to promise was an empty hope. Or worse, what I knew Mother in her heart of hearts thought was the truth about Serena—that all that legendary magic was, like the Wizard of Oz, a sham, a fraud, a lie.

II

There has always been a Serena in Mother's family, just as there's always been this legend about the beauty, wit, and wisdom of the family's women. And charm. Particularly charm.

There's a story floating around that Serena the First was a beautiful Quaker lady who was one of the few women romanced unsuccessfully by Ben Franklin. She was a Quaker, and she did marry into the family around the time of the Revolution. Beyond that, who knows? I do know this: If old Ben had met my grandmother, he'd have been smitten, all right: Gran with her pragmatism and her vision, her intelligence and her altruism and her charm.

"The exquisite Serena Van Zandt Harris," that's my gran. Or "the noted arts patron Serena Van Zandt Harris," or "Serena Van Zandt Harris, heiress of the Van Zandt mercantile and shipping fortune." Or "robber baron for-

*tune," depending on which magazine, financial paper, or
supermarket tabloid you happened to be reading.*

*As far back as I can remember, I've been conscious of the
power of Gran's charm.*

*"Gran shimmers," I said to Mother once when I was
little, too little to understand the look that crossed Mom's
face, or why she grabbed me and hugged me hard.*

*I know now that Gran's charm and power lie in the still
center that's inside Gran's outside layer of shimmering energy. A layer that's like the nacre on a pearl. Serena—for
Gran it's an appropriate name.*

*I know a couple of other things, too. Such charm and
power as Gran has can be addictive. People flock to her
aura like moths to flame. I realize now how hard it must
have been for Mother to wrench herself free. I know that's
why Mom really took off for England, rather than going
to Vredezucht this summer. She didn't want to wake that
struggle in herself again.*

*I know something else. I'm vulnerable to addiction, too.
Oh, not to the kind of things we're afraid Sophie's addicted
to. And I certainly hope not to what Mom calls chemistry
and Aunt Rena, all too often, calls earth-shattering love.
Maybe not even addiction to Gran's charisma—I haven't
been around her long enough yet to know. But addiction
to life in the circle of quiet she creates.*

The road I'd turned into was a country one, not very
wide, lined with old maples and here and there a small,

Norman Rockwell kind of house. Not the kind Dad designs, which are modern, but more like the ones in Sinclair Lewis's *Main Street,* which we read last year in English class. Mother, who's a great admirer of Lewis, would look at this street and murmur, "Suffocating," beneath her breath.

Out of the blue, I was glad she wasn't here. And I wasn't feeling apprehensive anymore.

The road had opened onto a village green. All around it great willow trees sighed softly, and houses of dove-colored wood, houses of pale cut stone, stood where they'd stood for a century and a half behind foaming flowers. In the pearly twilight the houses glowed. The lawns glowed emerald, and the flowers were the luminous shades of the Chinese porcelains my Grandmother Blair collects. I'm no expert on early United States architecture, but I've been exposed to Dad's influence enough to know that the design of these was good. Not flashy, not rustic, just very, very good.

Mom and Dad took me to Williamsburg, Virginia, once, some years ago. The green here made me think of the Palace Green. Only instead of a redbrick governor's palace at the far end, there was a white clapboard church. Instead of catalpa trees around the green there were the willows. And the green itself was not just grass. There were beds of flowers, carefully laid out and neatly edged in boxwood. The neatness and order, the way things glowed, reminded me so strongly of Gran.

All of a sudden a peal of bells began to ring from the church steeple. All of a sudden my eyes were filled with tears.

When I blinked them clear, I felt as if I'd been transported to Disneyland. Coming down the lefthand road was a gaily painted surrey. A scarlet fringe edged its canopy, and there were scarlet tassels on the fly net of the gray horse.

Nobody but Walt Disney or my grandmother Serena would have plunked that horse and surrey down in the middle of late twentieth-century Pennsylvania. But the driver of the surrey was strictly from prime-time TV. He could have been a Tom Selleck clone, but was golden-haired and younger. Just-out-of-college age. Wait till Sophie gets a load of *that,* I thought, and was surprised at the feelings the thought stirred in me.

I guess I *didn't* know myself so well.

The surrey was coming toward me, and I slowed as I reached it and leaned out the window.

"Excuse me, can you tell me which of these is Mrs. Harris's house?"

"They're all her houses. If you mean the house she lives in, it's that gray stone house on the far side of the church." He leaned forward, looking at me closely, and his face split slowly in a grin.

"You're one of the granddaughters she's expecting, aren't you? I'm Carl Lindstrom, Serena Van Zandt's resident archaeologist."

"I'm Laura Blair." To my intense embarrassment, I found myself gabbling. "I'm afraid Gran's not expecting me, not really, because Mom cabled we weren't coming. Only I just found out a couple of hours ago that I could, just me—I hope she's still going to have room for me . . ."

"Whoa, hold on! No, not you, Silver." Carl laughed as the horse turned a puzzled face. "One thing your grandmother's got plenty of around here is room. She'll be delighted to see you. You'll find her in the Potter's House."

He pointed with his light whip toward a small, two-story structure the color of a mourning dove, half hidden by trees across the green.

I thanked him and drove on slowly, my heart pounding.

I parked, quietly, before the building. Twilight had deepened now, and a soft glow of lamplight came from the open windows. The front door stood open as if it beckoned.

I went up the steps slowly, half in a trance. Something in the corner of my mind, that journalist's faculty I must have inherited from Mother, said, *This is going to be one of those moments you remember*. Remomberable, the faint, elusive, rhythmic squeak; rememberable, the scent of the pale pink roses that overhung the porch.

Rememberable, as if it were an old, Rembrandt kind of painting, the figure of my grandmother, on a low stool on the far side of the single room, bent like a madonna over the turning potter's wheel.

There were plain, long curtains of some filmy stuff that drifted in the breeze, and the few pieces of furniture were of old carved wood, lovingly polished. A spinet on one wall held brass candlesticks with a satin sheen, and the little humpbacked sofa was covered in flame-stitch embroidery. The jewel tones of the old needlework glowed.

And then there was Gran—Serena the legend, who drove Mother up the wall.

She didn't see me at first, for she was intent upon her work. Her thin, delicate hands curved lovingly over the little jar on the turning wheel. Her face in profile was chiseled, illusively young. The oil lamp on the side table cast a circle of light around her, like a halo on a medieval saint.

Nobody but Gran and Martha Graham could get away with wearing a ponytail at their ages. Gran's silver-frosted dark auburn hair hung down her back from a velvet ribbon high on her crown. The lamplight glinted on the heavy silver cross on its long chain, etched the folds of the printed caftan of Indian muslin. Crosses and caftans are practically Gran's trademarks; she refers to the caftans as "my blue jeans."

I didn't make a sound, but Gran felt my presence. She looked up, her face lightening. And then she was hurrying toward me, her slender, slightly stooped figure seeming taller than it was, her misty aquamarine eyes aglow.

"Laura? Oh, my dear child, I'm so glad to see you! So your parents changed their minds, after all!"

"No, they didn't." I swallowed. "It's just me, Gran."

She put her arms around me, light as a butterfly's wings, but I could feel her slightness and her closeness. Then she held me off and looked at me, and nodded slightly, as though in affirmation of something she'd been thinking. Then she kissed my forehead.

"Welcome to Vredezucht, Laura."

Laura Serena, something in me almost said. I shook my head in faint disbelief. Was I succumbing to the spell already?

I shook my head to clear it. "Gran, I had no idea you were doing so much here," I said dazedly.

Gran blushed like a girl. "I didn't dare tell anybody the whole truth ahead of time," she confessed. "First, because I knew exactly what your mother and Rena would say. Second, because I wanted it to be a secret until I was ready to open it to the public."

"Some secret," I said giddily. "You even have your own resident archaeologist?"

Gran's eyes twinkled. "He's a dish, isn't he? On loan to me from some highly important graduate school or other. Anyway," she reverted to her earlier subject, "yes, the restored buildings will be open to the public. Not on the scale of Williamsburg. But the Van Zandts built this town; it's a piece of our American past. And since, as your mother would say, it's 'downright wicked for one family to take that much *out* of the general public without giving something *back*,' this town is my newest contribution. I hope it'll encourage children to take more of an interest in history," she added practically.

"I'll bet it will." I grinned. I could take a fair guess at the extent of Gran's magic making. "When do the thundering hordes arrive?"

"Over the Fourth of July," Gran said. "That's the official opening with assorted bigwigs." And the press, invited or otherwise, I added mentally. "There'll be a special invitation-only tour on my birthday, for personal friends. And, of course, the family."

"Are they here yet?"

"Not the overseas contingent, except for my sister Alexandra—she came last week. She's staying with me, and right now she's taking a nap. Lisa and Beth came yesterday. I don't know when Rena's getting in! She's phoned four times so far, so excited I couldn't make out one word she was saying."

"Count your blessings," I said darkly.

Gran chuckled. "Sophie again? Or has your Aunt Rena gotten married again while my back was turned? No, she couldn't, could she? The current divorce isn't final." She shook her head. "I asked her last time why she persists in marrying at her age, and Rena gave me one of those poignant looks of hers and said, 'Mother, I am an old-fashioned woman. I believe in *marrying* the man I love.' Isn't it unfortunate she loves so many!"

I grinned. "You should hear what Mom says on the subject!"

"I can imagine," Gran said dryly. "Speaking of your mother, did she really get a book contract this time? Or is she holding her grandfather's fortune against me, again? Or is it the usual claustrophobia she gets at the bare thought of a family reunion? Or is it something else this time?"

Something in my throat tightened. Maybe it was the dust from the clay in the room, but all at once it was hard to breathe.

I didn't know I'd turned away or made a sound, until my grandmother's hand touched me lightly.

"Laura, it's all right. It's *all right*. You don't have to tell me about it unless you want to. I'm just very glad you're here. Now I must go home and make sure your Great-Aunt Alexandra is awake. Dinner will be at my house in an hour, but come whenever you're ready. You can't miss it. It's the house with the lace curtains, right beyond the church."

I gulped and wiped my eyes. "Where . . . where do you want me to stay?"

"Right here," Gran said. "Lisa and Beth are in the house next door, so you won't be lonely."

She kissed me, and left, and I walked slowly up the narrow, winding stairs.

At the top was a small landing with bookshelves and a child's trundle bed and a cradle, and beyond it one square room, a duplicate of the one downstairs. It had slanted walls, a fireplace, and a high four-poster bed with a crocheted coverlet. There was a photograph on the wall of a young girl with a mystical expression and my own firm chin. Gran's mother, my great-grandmother . . . I threw myself down on the bed and lay there with my arms behind my head, trying to swallow the lump in my throat. Presently I got up and unpacked. I found the old-fashioned bathroom and took a bath in a footed tub long enough to lie down in. There wasn't any shower, but there were bath towels the size of sheets. That was a good thing, because when I was just climbing out there was a commotion downstairs, and a minute later the bathroom door banged open without ceremony.

"Wait a minute!" I yelled, grabbing a towel. Then I did a double-take. "Sophie, what in blue blazes are you supposed to be done up as?"

"The latest thing on King's Road. I hope it'll knock the pants off Mummy, but Gran didn't bat an eye." Sophie preened, obviously pleased with my reaction. Her hair, by nature a light brown, was chopped off like a boy's on the left side and neon green. The right side was a wild orange lion's mane. The top stood straight up and was magenta. She was wearing a leather skirt that covered about as much of her as a bikini bottom, and a skin-tight black turtleneck knit top, a gold hipchain, and a safety pin in her left ear.

"I thought those were out now," I said dryly.

"They are, but this one's real gold, so I thought I'd hang on to it. Besides, it freaks Mummy out. You haven't seen her yet, have you?"

"Gran said she hadn't arrived."

"Good!" Sophie said fervently. "I want to avoid her bumping into us till we've had a chance to talk to you and Aunt Kay."

"Mom's not here. I thought you knew that. What do you mean, *we?*"

Sophie waved a hand toward the open door. A young man stood there, lounging negligently against the doorframe and dragging on a cigarette. His hair was a normal cut and color, almost black; he wore black leather jeans and a black turtleneck, and his eyes were very blue. As they met mine their sullenness changed to something much more personal.

Heat flooded through me, and I pulled the bath sheet tighter. Sophie giggled. "It's okay, it's all in the family. Laura, this is our cousin Jay Tremaine."

"H-how do you do?" I murmured weakly, and then turned an even deeper red at the stuffiness of that formal phrase.

Jay's blue eyes twinkled. "Just fine. In fact I'm starting to like—what do you call this town, Vredezucht?—more every minute."

His eyes traveled over me with unmistakable appreciation. I pulled the bath towel tighter. Sophie giggled.

"Vredezucht! It sounds like 'Really yuck!' Leave it to Serena to come up with an original name."

"It means 'place of peace,' 'breath of peace,' something like that. And it's been called that for a couple of hundred years." I was gabbling, and I knew it. And I knew darn well Sophie knew it, too, and knew why. I could cheerfully have throttled her.

"I think Laura would have appreciated a more conventional introduction," Jay said easily. There was a touch of laughter in his voice, just as if he'd read my mind. He touched Sophie's arm lightly. "Come on, let's give this poor girl a chance to get dressed." Over Sophie's head Jay's eyes met mine, in shared amusement and maybe something more. "See you again when you're decent," he called back teasingly as they turned to leave.

Decent! I thought, catching my breath as they clattered down the stairs. I wanted far more than that. I went back to my room, where my suitcase now waited, and began rapidly to root through my clothes. The new linen shift . . . I could hear Sophie's voice echoing my mother's: square. Ditto the pants and blazer. I pulled out the flowered voile I had intended to save for Gran's birthday party and jerked it on over the necessary full petticoat and chemise.

I remember thinking that the lace-trimmed under-garments, the filmy dress itself, went with this room. I remember looking at myself in the black-and-gold-framed mirror, the clouded glass giving back to me a reflection at once familiar and subtly changed. My hair curled slightly from the steam, and I didn't need blusher since my cheeks were flushed, but otherwise my face was very pale. The blues and greens of my dress brought out the color of my eyes, which were enormous.

I remember thinking of these things vaguely, and of Gran's birthday. But what I was really conscious of were other things entirely: The way my heart was pounding. The way my breath had caught when I had looked up into Jay Tremaine's blue eyes. And the sudden feeling I had of knowing and being known.

III

When I ran outside, ready to leave for Gran's, I found Aunt Lisa and Beth coming down the steps of the house next door.

"Laura! What a lovely surprise!" Aunt Lisa hurried over to hug me, and Beth followed. "When did your mother change her mind? Where is she?"

"In England. Dad's in Philadelphia on business. I'm here alone. His idea."

"Hmmmm," Aunt Lisa said shrewdly, "I want to hear all about it, but not now. This family reunion dinner's going to be exciting enough without having Kay as the subject for discussion."

It was going to be fancy—that at least was sure. Aunt Lisa was wearing an ankle-length dress, black and sheer and trimmed with lace. Her halo of loose red-gold curls made her look like a lady from a seventeenth-century portrait. Beth's dress was ankle-length, too, and looked a lot like a modern ballet outfit. That is, it was very plain and clinging on top, and it had a circle skirt. Beth looked very thin in it. Maybe that was because she'd gotten taller since I'd seen her last. She was very pale, and there were gray smudges around her eyes, and her hair was pulled up in a dancer's knot. I looked at her closely, and Beth caught my glance and looked away.

We walked across the green. Lights poured from all the windows of Gran's stone house to welcome us. The house was something. Dad would have loved it, I knew at once, even though it wasn't modern. It had what he called integrity and purity of line. There was a center hall, with a sweeping staircase and two rooms on each side. There were embroidered lace curtains at the tall open windows. There were gilt and crystal chandeliers and wall sconces, gilt-framed mirrors, and carved white woodwork.

Aunt Rena's unmistakable laughter had floated out to us as we approached. She was wearing something royal blue and sexy, and her makeup was as lavish as Sophie's, though more *Vogue* than punk. She looked as if she should have some gorgeous hunk hovering over her, but since she didn't she was coming on to Uncle Roger, even though he was over seventy and very dignified.

I'd only met him once before, when I was about six, and he'd looked just as old and just as dignified then. Actually he was our cousin, not our uncle, because he was Great-Aunt Alexandra's son. Sophie and Beth and I always referred to him as "Uncle Roger," just as we always spoke of "Great-Aunt Alexandra." It was expected, and it suited them. Uncle Roger was an art or antiques expert at some London gallery, and he looked the part, gray-haired, impeccably tailored, and very quiet.

The only other man in the room was Jay, also impeccably tailored, but with mischief lurking behind the sophistication in his eyes.

And then there was Gran. Gran in a very plain violet silk caftan adorned only with a heavy jewelled cross. Beside her, everybody else, even Aunt Rena, seemed somehow muted. Gran came across to greet us, holding out her hands. Gran tucked my arm through hers and led me over to greet Great-Aunt Alexandra, an exquisite old porcelain figurine with wrinkles instead of cracks, in a long dress and pearl choker and lots of glittering old-fashioned rings. Great-Aunt Alexandra was, believe it or not, a Serene Highness, because after Uncle Roger's father was killed she'd married a minor, now long dead, member of European royalty. She greeted me in a kind and very old-sounding voice.

"Alexandra, this is Laura. Isn't it lovely she could come, after all? Kay and Ken were both called off on some wildly exciting secret business projects and couldn't get away," Gran said, loud and firm enough for everybody in the room to get the message.

Liu, the elderly Chinese gentleman who's run Gran's

homes for simply centuries, came in to announce dinner. And I do mean we *dined*. Exactly what we ate I couldn't tell you, but it came in many courses and was fabulous. By the time dessert was over, we couldn't have eaten another bite.

Liu moved quietly around, removing dessert plates and refilling coffee cups. Candlelight flickered softly on the ebony and gold federal furniture, the small gold-edged, jewel-colored cups. Gran leaned forward slightly, clasped her hands beneath her chin, and gazed around at her assembled family. The sleeves of her violet caftan fell back, revealing their turquoise lining. Her aquamarine eyes sparkled.

"Now!" Gran said. "Now here's our plan!"

A current of air seemed to travel around the table, touching each of us in turn. And Gran proceeded to unfold a program that would have daunted Disneyland and worn out people half her age.

Gran had bought the old Van Zandt houses, some tumbledown barns and what had once been crafts shops, and a down-at-the-heels hotel and row of stores. She'd taken them over, stripped off the grime of years, and polished them lovingly. I gathered that two years ago Vredezucht had been on the way to becoming a ghost town, and that the few hundred families still living there had been delighted to have the place saved.

Gran distributed beautiful illustrated maps, and an equally lovely brochure of photographs. I stole a look at them as Gran's voice went on, describing the schedule of events for now through the Fourth of July, and I was dazzled. Gran hadn't merely restored old houses. She had reconstructed the crafts cottages, a schoolhouse, and a mill. She had duplicated an old factory building from some other Van Zandt roosting place, and eventually it would house conferences and seminars and special programs. There was an Opera House. There was a little art museum, and an archaeological center, and in a former stable a museum of early United States costumes and life. There were barns, and gardens, and a model farm, and farm animals.

The evening broke up very late, after a last treat of cookies and lemonade in Gran's yellow drawing room, and firm instructions for us to meet her on the green at nine A.M. for her personally escorted grand tour. Great-Aunt Alexandra was the only relative staying the night beneath Gran's own roof. Aunt Rena and Sophie had been put—appropriately for Aunt Rena—in one of the grander houses, and Uncle Roger and Jay were at the Monongahela House. Uncle Roger invited the aunts back to the Monongahela House with him and Jay for "something more spirited than lemonade, perhaps." Jay invited Sophie and me, with Beth as an afterthought. Somewhat to my surprise, Sophie shook her head.

"You can forget us. It's been a long evening! We'll see you in the morning, ducks."

So Jay went off with the other three toward the hotel, and Sophie linked her arms through Beth's and mine. "I'll walk you home. I could use some air," she said when the others were out of earshot. "Gorblimey, if that Buckingham Palace dinner party had gone on much longer, I'd have gone bonkers!"

I giggled. "It wasn't quite that bad!"

"Wasn't it? I felt like I ought to curtsey and back out of the room after Great-Aunt Alexandra gave me her hand to kiss. 'Great-Aunt Alexandra,' for pity's sake. It's positively Victorian," Sophie said, shaking her multicolored hair in the moonlight.

"I think it's sweet. Anyway, nobody could accuse you of being Victorian," I told Sophie severely.

"Thanks for that. I still feel suffocated," said Sophie the unsquelchable.

"I feel silly," Beth announced. Suddenly she kicked off her shoes and thrust them in my hands. "Here, hold these, will you?"

Before we knew what she was up to, she threw herself into three perfect cartwheels and fetched up in front of us, breathless.

"My cousin, the ballerina," I teased.

"Our cousin, the little kid, you mean. You're acting like you're six years old, Elizabeth, and whatever would Serena say?" Sophie, wickedly, put on a Great-Aunt Alexandra face.

"Gran can't see us in the dark, silly! And when I was

six, I didn't turn cartwheels. I always had to be careful not to turn my ankle or skin my knees, on account of dance recitals." Beth turned a couple of more cartwheels and grinned at us in triumph.

"She *is* feeling silly. Maybe it's midsummer madness. I've never seen the child like this before, have you, Laura?" Sophie took a firm grip on Beth's arm and steered her toward Wisteria Cottage. "In her mum's absence I'd better see her up to her crib. See you tomorrow, Laura."

We separated to walk to our dark houses through the warm June dark.

It felt weird, going into the Potter's House alone. I'd never stayed in a house by myself before. And I hadn't thought to leave any lights on when I went out. I groped for a switch on the wall beside the door, and the electrified oil lamp across the room threw out its circle of light.

The potter's wheel stood out in high relief, the little jar Gran had been working on still standing there forlornly.

It should have been wrapped with wet paper towels, I knew that much. Gran must have been in a dither, underneath her surface calm. I explored till I found a little kitchenette, and soaked paper towels beneath the faucet, and wrapped them around the jar. Then I found a piece of plastic by the potter's wheel and put that around it, too.

The house was so still. Outside, somewhere distant, an owl hooted.

I'd promised to check in with Dad, I remembered. And I'd seen a phone by the bed . . . I went up, undressed, crawled in beneath lace-trimmed sheets fragrant with lavender, and called.

Dad answered at once. "I was getting worried."

"Everything's fine! I only just got loose from Gran's family dinner party, that's all."

Dad chuckled. "How is everybody?"

"Fine. Sophie's got tricolored hair . . . Dad, what about Mom? Can I call her? Do I tell her that I'm here?"

There was a pause. "Better let things lay," Dad said at last. "You can write her all about it after you get home."

"Sophie said she wasn't at the bed-and-breakfast."

"She's probably very busy doing research," Dad said. "Laura, the job here's going to take longer than I expected. I'll call you and let you know my plans as soon as I've made them. In the meantime, call me here at night any time you need me. Give your grandmother my love. Good night, honey."

He hung up. I lay awake in the unfamiliar dark, listening to the owl and thinking how much Mother would love it here, if she'd just let herself.

I awoke to squirrels playing tag on the roof outside my window and the sound of voices in the street outside. I ran to the window. Sophie and Jay were standing there, patting Silver. Or rather Jay was scratching the horse's ears while Sophie came on, full voltage, to Carl Lindstrom. He had a quizzical, amused expression on his face. He looked up, saw me, and waved, and then Jay waved, too. Sophie put on a big smile and yelled up to me, "See you later, luv," and hauled Jay firmly into the surrey with her. They all jounced off around the green toward Gran's.

I pulled on jeans and a shirt and went downstairs.

There was a little kitchenette off the main room, stocked with basics and some luscious croissants. I was filling the coffeepot at the sink when I saw Beth waving vigorously at me from the porch next door. I went out on my own porch, and Beth called, "Come over! Mom's cooking breakfast."

"I've got croissants."

"So have we—two for each of us. Bring yours with you." Beth disappeared, and I got my two croissants and went on over.

Their house was called Wisteria Cottage, and it was larger than the Potter's House. Two bedrooms and a bath upstairs; a living room, dining room, and kitchen down. The furniture, Aunt Lisa said, was Shaker. "It's always been very popular in this part of the country. So practical. Get the chairs down, girls." Aunt Lisa nodded to where they were hanging on the wall. She was at the stove, in a silk kimono with a French chef's apron over it, scrambling eggs. I giggled.

" 'Portrait of the Artist as a French Chef'?"

"Portrait of a mother who's learned from experience that silk's impractical," Aunt Lisa said promptly.

We ate the eggs, which were good, and the croissants, which were definitely going to be murder to everybody's figure. "I could get addicted," I said dreamily, with my first bite. "Oh, well, we can work it off making the rounds this morning with Gran."

"Don't remind me," Aunt Lisa groaned.

Beth emerged from her shell of silence. "Mom! It will be fun."

"Of course it will," Aunt Lisa said promptly. "I grew up following your grandmother around through museums, remember? This 'little tour' will turn out to be pure magic. It'll also be exhausting. And we'll all get so swept up in the spirit that we'll later come to discover we've committed ourselves to all sorts of activities. I can just see an art assignment for those blessed brochures looming up before me!"

"The brochures are all printed," Beth pointed out.

"Are they? What about museum handbooks? And graphics for press releases, et cetera?" Aunt Lisa laughed. "Kay knew exactly what she was doing when she took off for England!" Then she looked at me, laughed again, and hugged me. "You two girls are safe, at least. I haven't heard anything so far about Mother staging a ballet, and if she did she'd probably bring in the Ballet Theatre! And none of us know yet what your particular talents are, do we, Laura? The cousins will probably be drafted to hand out programs or something for the grand opening, but in the meantime, sweetie, you go ahead and enjoy. Just don't let yourself get swept away!"

Out of my unconscious, a picture of Jay Tremaine lounging in the doorway leaped into my mind. I saw his eyes looking at me with familiarity and admiration, and felt myself turning scarlet.

Aunt Lisa laughed again and kissed the top of my head, and Beth looked at me gravely.

Everybody managed to make it to Gran's designated meeting place on time—even Aunt Rena, wearing five-inch spike heels. Somewhere between the schoolhouse and the farmyard she'd broken a heel, and from then on she limped fetchingly.

Sophie wasn't doing a bad job of clutching Jay, without any such excuse. Not that he minded. I felt myself growing quiet at first, then more and more bubbly, just like Mother does. I could have kicked myself. Then I thought about what all of that signified and could have kicked myself some more.

"Don't let it get you," Beth muttered, coming up beside me as Jay and Sophie, so entwined they couldn't walk a straight line, wandered ahead of us through the costume exhibit, mocking out the decorous period clothing.

"I don't know what you mean."

"Yes, you do." Beth's eyes were grave. "He's gorgeous, and there's chemistry between you. He's showing off for your benefit, you know."

"Don't be silly," I said shortly.

"He is. He keeps looking to see if you're watching, and you are." I felt myself growing hot, and Beth added quickly, "Don't worry, nobody else notices. They're all too wrapped up in their own problems." Beth shook her head. "Poor Gran! She's building her Garden of Eden, and everybody's brought a private serpent in."

"Except Gran. Gran doesn't have one."

"Yes, she does. The fact that none of the rest of us share her visions. Oh, we love Gran, and we think what she does is wonderful, but not as wonderful as if it were done by somebody else!" Beth paused, searching for words. "Her light's too bright," she said at last.

"For you?" I asked gently, after another pause.

"I'm not talking about me. Look at your mom. Look at Aunt Rena. The only talent *she* has is a talent for turning men on, and we all know how that's worked out. Did you see my mother's face last night when we walked into Gran's drawing room and she saw her portrait of Gran hanging there?"

"It's a lovely portrait."

"Sure, it is. Mother's won prizes and sold to museums. But in Gran's house her work hangs next to a Rembrandt. Mother's not a Rembrandt, and she knows it."

"But that's silly!" I said, appalled. "Gran didn't mean there to be a comparison. She's proud of Aunt Lisa!"

"She's proud of all of us. That doesn't mean we don't make the comparisons ourselves, does it?"

"Is that the serpent *you've* brought in with you?" I asked softly.

"It's all of us. Oh, there's Uncle Roger. I want to ask him something." Beth hurried away.

I stood looking at the tableau of *A Social Assembly in the 1830s,* gathering my thoughts.

"We ought to offer to do some Living Pictures like this for Serena's birthday celebration," a voice said at my shoulder. "That flowery number on the left wouldn't look half bad on you."

I spun around. Jay was standing there, smiling at me. "Of course, it would be kind of a shame to cover you up with all that fabric. You have great legs, as I remember." His eyes twinkled.

"Let's just forget about the conditions we met under, shall we?" I said with as much dignity as I could manage.

Jay drew his finger across his mouth. "My lips are sealed. But I won't promise not to remember! Now what do you think about my brilliant suggestion? I give my solemn word I won't suggest we dramatize the family history to date, so you don't have to worry about any bathtub scenes!"

"I haven't the foggiest idea what you're talking about. Living Pictures, that is," I added hastily.

"They were all the rage at the time of Serena the Third. Scenes from books or plays, or history, like at Madame Tussaud's waxworks or these scenes here. Only with human beings holding the poses, instead of store window dummies. Seriously," Jay said, looking anything but serious, "throwing together a Living Picture stunt for the gala wouldn't be a bad idea. The last I saw Aunt Serena, she was deep in consultation with some musician over the program for the entertainment Wednesday evening. Seems she's got a lot of VIPs flying in. And here I thought we all were the important people that were coming." His smile removed any rudeness from his words.

I smiled, too, ruefully. "You don't know Gran! Family's terribly important to her, but so is 'sharing one's gifts and talents with the world.' "

"Too bad I don't have any talent to share!" Jay said lightly. Then his voice sobered. "You're right, I don't know her at all. She's really something, isn't she?" As if betrayed into sentimentality, he went on smoothly, "So how about the Living Pictures? Shall we volunteer?"

"What somebody ought to volunteer for is a scene from *A Midsummer Night's Dream*. Nothing like being relevant! But I'm not an actress. Why don't you ask Sophie?"

"Sophie," Jay said, "thinks Shakespeare is a drag." He tucked my arm firmly through his. "Come on, let's catch up with Aunt Serena."

We saw the surrey and ran to catch up with it, hoping Gran was inside. Instead, it held Aunt Rena, nursing her twisted ankle and spreading her charm around to Carl and Uncle Roger. She waved gaily to us, and they rolled on.

I stumbled over a rock in the unpaved path and caught at Jay. He put his arms around me to right me, and when I once again had my balance he did not take them away.

When we did catch up with Gran, a good while later, she was thrilled about the idea of the Living Pictures. What was more, she left them all up to me.

IV

Journal—Thursday, June 23

Midsummer's Eve. Longest day of the year, the summer solstice, magic time. That's Gran's real birthday.

Gran, being Gran, thinks nothing of altering the calendar. The big party's set for Saturday. That's so poor ordinary mortals who hold down jobs will have a whole day free for the revels.

I can just hear Mom's voice saying that, with her little laugh.

I thought I was going to be here in Vredezucht on my own, but I was wrong. All the time Gran was showing us around, it was like Mom's and Dad's voices were holding a dialogue in my head: Dad saying, "Kay, be fair. You get sore as the dickens when you think Serena doesn't consider people's job commitments." Mom, giving that airy shoulder shrug that makes people melt and saying lightly, "Serena and the Queen of England! One birthday's not

47

enough for them, they have two—the real and the official!"

Mom. I feel guilty about not telling her I'm here. Not to mention feeling worried about her. Oh, sure, unless Dad's told her, she wouldn't know to call me here. But usually she's as good about keeping in touch as she's bad about writing letters, and she's fantastic about being able to track people down anywhere on the globe. If she really wants to. Or unless something's wrong. My mother the journalist is also my mother the flake. She's exactly the kind of person to get herself kidnapped as a hostage in a foreign airport.

She'd probably think it was a great scoop.

. . . Laura Serena Blair, come off it! One, she's only been gone nine days. Two, you wanted to get out from under thinking about—all that—didn't you?

Think about something nicer. Think about Jay.

. . . on second thought, maybe I'd better not let my mind get obsessed in that *direction, either . . . !*

That Gran's party was to be held on Saturday meant I had two days to dream up those Living Pictures. When we finally caught up with Gran on Thursday morning, in the Opera House, Jay promptly spilled the beans. Gran gave us a vague, radiant smile, murmured, "What a wonderful idea, darlings," and turned back to explaining to a man from New York's Lincoln Center how even small towns, at the end of the nineteenth century, used to have opera houses (sized and shaped like a grange hall, with an auditorium downstairs and a ballroom with parlor organ or player piano up) for visiting road shows to appear in.

As we dutifully trailed in Gran's wake through the barns, the livery stable, and the crafts workshop where Carl was planing the surface of a beautiful old Pembroke table, Jay kept whispering suggestions for Living Pictures in my ear. His suggestions got progressively sillier, and it was great fun. Later, back at Gran's for lunch, we continued the game. Jay and I took our plates of cold chicken and potato salad down by the river bank, and Sophie and Beth joined us in dangling our feet in the placid water, and the ideas for the Living Pictures got sillier yet—particularly once Sophie was there.

"Mummie can be a visiting opera singer. Can't you picture her in black velvet and Great-Aunt Alexandra's dirty old diamonds? Only it ought to be a real performance, not just a Living Picture. Except that Mummie can't carry a tune."

"That wouldn't stop her. Rena would flash the family smile and everybody in the audience would go tone deaf with joy," Jay commented, polishing off his last dill pickle and reaching for one of mine.

"Beth can be—who was it, that famous dancer P.T. Barnum used to cart around? Pavlova?" Sophie rolled her eyes in Beth's direction. "Can you be a dying swan, Bets? Not to be rude, but frankly you look like you could do it without makeup, ducks."

"No," Beth said flatly.

Sophie did a double-take. "Sorry! Didn't mean to offend. Why don't you be a dance-hall girl instead? Liven up this hick town. I've got a bustier and crinoline I got in London that would be perfect—"

"*I said no,*" Beth interrupted tightly.

I decided a change of subject was required. "Jay could be—what did they use to call them? Stage Door Johnnies?" I giggled.

"Too right." Sophie laughed loudly, but her eyes weren't laughing. Then she gave a hoot and proposed a decidedly disrespectful act for Gran and Great-Aunt Alexandra together, and the mood lightened.

After lunch Jay proposed canoeing on the river.

"Sounds a right treat, but I'm for my bikini first. Don't want to ruin me best togs, do I?" Sophie, having been relatively prim and proper all through lunch, was now at her most Cockney.

"Me, too," I said ungrammatically, and Beth and Sophie and I split to change into bathing suits. I got back to the river before the other two and found Jay swimming.

"Dive in!" he called. "It's deep enough along here." So I did. We swam and talked, or rather Jay teased me and I blushed a lot and felt light-headed. Finally Sophie appeared, in the bare minimum of a hot pink bikini. She dove in, too, and surfaced like a seal beside us.

"Where've you been?" I asked. "We've been waiting for ages."

"Didn't put a damper on your fun and games, did it?" Sophie asked knowingly. "Or was our dear cousin here coming on too strong?"

"Where's Beth?" I interrupted hastily.

"I haven't the foggiest. You want I should go find her? I thought I saw her cutting through the woods as I was coming."

"I'll go. You haven't had a chance to swim, so you wait here for her. Jay can go get the canoes." I scrambled out, half needing a chance to be alone and half worrying a little about Beth. It wasn't like her just not to appear.

I cut through the woodland in the direction Sophie suggested, and then I saw her: Beth, the way I'd never seen her. She was in a dark bathing suit cut like a leotard, with a circular jersey wrap skirt tied over it, and she was happy. It struck me that I'd never seen her when she was this happy, dancing barefoot in a glade of filtered sunlight. It wasn't ballet dancing, and it wasn't dancing for an audience. It was just for herself and the bright-eyed squirrel watching from a tree stump. Beth looked lit up from within, like a Christmas ornament.

For a minute I was afraid to break the spell. Then I backed off some, behind a tree, and called out, "Beth! Where are you?"

The inside light went out, and Beth stopped dancing. "Here," she called back in an ordinary voice. Presently she came out of the clearing, her feet thrust back into sandals and her face shuttered.

"Jay's getting the canoes," I said briskly. "We were kind of worried."

"I got distracted. I'm sorry I kept you waiting," Beth said briefly.

We went back to the river, where Jay and Sophie were readying the canoes. Jay took Beth in his, which was nice of him, and Sophie and I took the other. I was glad Dad had taught me how to paddle a canoe during vacations at Wisconsin lakes. We went down the river to near the falls, and then back upstream as far as the art museum. Then Aunt Lisa spotted us and said it was time we cleaned up for dinner.

Everyone was supposed to eat at Gran's again, but we cousins had all had more than enough family reunion and Van Zandt formality. Jay proposed we go somewhere to eat on our own, and Gran agreed. So we did, in Mom's old car, with Jay driving. He was not the world's safest driver, and the Chinese food we ended up eating was pretty pathetic, but neither of those things got to me as much as they usually would have. I was either going through a culture shock or a time lag. Or maybe just having fun with a boy who was different from any I'd ever known.

This time I remembered to leave some lamps lit, so I didn't come back to a gloomy house. Dad phoned soon after I got in. Gran had been calling him, trying to talk him into coming for her birthday (he couldn't) and the Fourth of July (he would). He hadn't heard from Mother, but he'd reached the London office of her publisher and left word about where each of us was. The editor there had seen her and was very enthusiastic about her (which figured), so I could stop worrying.

So when I put out my light, there was nothing on my mind except the Living Pictures. And Jay. I concentrated on the former, and it didn't take me long to realize that while the idea might have been great, it was also way too big. At least Gran isn't counting on them, I thought drowsily, and went to sleep.

The next thing I knew, it was broad daylight, and the smell of coffee and bacon was drifting up the stairs. Not from next door, either. I pulled on my robe and wandered down.

Jay was standing at the kitchen stove, expertly flipping pancakes. "Pull up a chair. Fresh-squeezed orange juice waiting, and I even managed to find some genuine Vermont maple syrup in Aunt Serena's pantry. Are you impressed?"

"I'm impressed to see you out this early. I had you figured for the type who'd stay out all night and then sleep till noon."

"Oh, I'm full of surprises. I can do lots of things when they really interest me!" Jay's hand touched my back lightly, then moved away as if the contact had perhaps been accidental. "I talked to Aunt Serena last night. She's looking forward to the Living Pictures. So I told Beth and Sophie to report here at ten for making plans. That gives us an hour first for breakfast."

Things were moving too fast. "You could at least have invited them for breakfast, since you're cooking," I said weakly.

"This was a last-minute inspiration. For the two of us," Jay said coolly. "They can feed themselves."

When Beth came, promptly at ten, Aunt Lisa was with her. "Don't mind me, I'm just going to sit here on the porch and plan a painting," Aunt Lisa said, settling comfortably into a wicker rocker. Beth gave her a sideways glance. I had a pretty strong idea that Aunt Lisa had come only to make sure that Beth did.

Sophie showed up twenty minutes late. "I suppose you've got everything set by now. What did you put me down for?" she asked unrepentantly.

"Nothing's set. Sit down and put your creativity to some good use for a change." Jay eyed Sophie's hair, which today had turned to an even yellow-green, as Sophie plopped herself on the porch steps.

By noon, when Carl drove up in the surrey to say Gran was expecting us at once for lunch, the planning session had degenerated into a repetition of yesterday's silliness. Carl looked at Beth, who was staring remotely into space, and at my two other cousins, who were laughing hysterically at each other's witticisms, and said, with an almost deliberate lack of emphasis, "Mrs. Van Zandt's really looking forward to this entertainment of yours, you know."

"Mrs. Van Zandt—that's a hoot!" Sophie blew a wisp of green hair from her face. "She never did officially ditch Grandpop, did she? And she's long past being *Miss* Van Zandt. I suppose *Ms.* wouldn't be traditional enough to suit Her Highness, so she's known to the world as *Mrs!*

"Sophie," Aunt Lisa said deliberately, "go. Right now. You and Beth and Jay ride over to your grandmother's with Carl. And please, as a favor to this traditional old aunt, wash some of that war paint off before lunch. It's enough to spoil the appetite of anyone over thirty. Laura and I will join you in a few minutes."

"What was that all about?" I asked when they had gone.

Aunt Lisa shrugged. "Beth could do with a breather from me, and some contact with those two may wake her up a bit. Laura, what are you going to do about these Living Pictures?"

I goggled at her. "What am *I* going to do?"

"You heard me. More to the point, you heard Carl. Mother's really touched that you came up with the idea, and it would be embarrassing for her if it fell through." *Or went poorly* was implicit in her tone. "At dinner last night, she was telling those men from Lincoln Center and the Smithsonian what a treat they had in store."

My heart sank. "Wait a minute! It wasn't *my* idea. Well, not all mine."

"Oh, Jay!" Aunt Lisa dismissed him with a shrug. "I wouldn't trust him with responsibility any more than I would my sister Rena. No, Laura, I'm afraid it's up to you."

"I don't know where to start," I said weakly.

"My first thought is Mother's scrapbooks. She has them, you know, scrapbooks and files of Van Zandt history back to when the first three came over from Holland in 1628. And my second thought is Carl Lindstrom. He's a cultural anthropologist or something, isn't he? Besides, he's the one you'll have to go through to get hold of the props and costumes. My third thought is, *you* make a list of scenes you can put together easily. There needn't be many, just a dozen or so. And *you* decide who'll be who." Aunt Lisa saw the expression on my face and laughed. "Don't worry! I'll talk the rest of the family into participating, too, so you'll have enough people. And I'll sketch the scenes for you, if you like, so you can refer to them when you're posing us."

The battle was lost, and I knew it. "Why me?" I asked weakly. Aunt Lisa laughed and hugged me.

"Because it was your idea, and a good one, and I'm not going to let Jay and Sophie spoil it for you. I could take over, but it will mean a lot more to Mother if it's done by you. You want my advice, do your research this afternoon without telling anyone, and I'll come over here before dinner to help you plan the poses. Then at dinner you just announce the rehearsal for tomorrow morning. Everyone will have had enough togetherness by then and will be glad of something new to do. And it will keep Mother from running us all ragged!"

"I know what you mean. I'm beginning to understand Mom's point of view a little better," I said ruefully.

"It's a little hard to catch one's breath around Serena sometimes," Aunt Lisa agreed. She paused. "Speaking of Kay, have you heard anything from her?"

"She's running around London, working very hard and loving it." If my answer was misleading, maybe I meant it to be. I had a feeling I didn't fool Aunt Lisa. She said, "Hmmm," cryptically.

We had lunch on Gran's screened porch, quite a formal lunch with a few more newly arrived distinguished guests. After lunch, taking Aunt Lisa's advice, I drifted off unobtrusively.

My first stop was the crafts workshop, where several artisans were busily working and Carl was applying a final coat of wax to the Pembroke table. "Lovely piece, isn't it? Belonged to your great-great-grandfather," he greeted me. "Or aren't you particularly interested in antiques?" From the twinkle in his eyes, I had a feeling he too had had his fill of Jay's and Sophie's fooling.

"Right now I'd better be interested," I said.

Carl nodded. "The Living Pictures? I've been expecting you." He looked at my face and laughed as Aunt Lisa had. "Don't look so worried! You don't have to do them at the Opera House, you know! Just in your grandmother's double parlor. She's already spoken to me about rigging some lights, and I've persuaded her that kerosene lamps as footlights would be more appropriate. Just stand your ground on what you want, and don't let that horde of relatives run roughshod over you, and you'll do fine."

"The problem is, I don't *know* what I want. I don't suppose I could just duplicate the dioramas in the museum, could I?"

Carl shook his head. "They're all set up for the grand tour. But we do have sketches for some additional scenes, for which the backdrops haven't yet been painted. Some of the clothing we'll be using in them is already in the workshop, and I can round up props. Anything else you'd need is probably in your grandmother's attic."

"Aunt Lisa suggested I check Serena's scrapbooks."

"Another good idea. Your grandmother will be out of the house all afternoon; she's taking those museum people for a drive. Now let me show you the sketches and costumes I spoke of."

By the time we'd spent a companionable, hard-working hour together, my spirits were considerably lifted.

When at last I headed back toward the village green, a well-filled notebook beneath my arm, I found Aunt Lisa sitting beneath a willow tree painting a water color of the Van Zandt House.

"My birthday present for Mother," she announced. "I'm getting in a couple of peaceful hours on it while the mob's away. How are you making out, honey?"

"Fine! I'm on my way to check out those scrapbooks. Is everybody gone?"

"Everyone but my daughter, and I don't know *where* she is." Aunt Lisa's face altered. "Laura? Has Beth talked to you?"

I shook my head.

"Then talk to her, will you? Please."

"About what?"

"That's the whole point. I don't know." Aunt Lisa rinsed her brush off, dried it, and laid it down. "You've seen her, Laura. Elizabeth's always been . . . reserved. But this is different. Almost as if she's afraid of something. She won't confide in me. She may in you."

I remembered that scratched-out letter, and the jolt I'd gotten when I first saw Beth two days ago. I didn't say so, not with Aunt Lisa looking as worried as she did right now. "Everybody's got problems this summer," I said lightly.

"How about you?"

"Me? I'm fine! I was thinking about Sophie."

I went on across the green to Gran's house.

It was very quiet now in the late afternoon. The shutters were half closed, and the gilt and crystal seemed to slumber in the dimness. A faint breeze riffled the sheer curtains, but the air seemed still. I realized, sharply, how much of the energy in Gran's world came straight from her. In her absence, everything sank into half-life, waiting.

Liu came to greet me and brought out the scrapbooks. There were many, bound in gilt-touched leather, in crimson and green and blue. He piled them on the bare polished dining room table, and showed me where the files were, hidden behind secret doors in the paneling.

I started with the scrapbooks, and pretty soon I was in a daze. I didn't even hear Liu come back in. "Tea is served in the drawing room," he murmured and withdrew discreetly. Leave it to Liu to be formal, but if he'd gone to all that trouble, I didn't have the heart to disappoint him. I went into the drawing room, and there was Great-Aunt Alexandra, in black lace and her "dirty old diamonds," gazing helplessly at an ornate silver tea set.

She looked at me vaguely. Then the faded eyes brightened. "Lisa? How nice."

"It's Laura, Great-Aunt Alexandra. Kay's daughter," I added, as the eyes turned doubtful.

"Oh . . . yes. Of course." Great-Aunt Alexandra

nodded, but I would have bet she didn't remember my mother, either. "Shall I pour for you, Great-Aunt?" I asked gently.

"If you would be so kind."

I poured and, at Great-Aunt Alexandra's instruction, added milk and two spoons of sugar. I put poppyseed cake and linzer cookies on a porcelain dessert plate and set it carefully at Great-Aunt Alexandra's elbow. She sat there sipping tea like a good little girl and nodding to me politely. She could have been one of the figures in the museum, come to life. To half-life. At last, in desperation, I began to tell her about the Living Pictures I was working on for Gran's birthday party. To my astonishment, she suddenly began to sparkle.

"But how charming! Serena will be so pleased. We used to have Living Pictures very often years ago, you know, Serena and our brother William and I. Mama used to love them, and so did Papa. Particularly the Fourth of July that William and I did *Scenes from the Life of Washington*. That was the last Fourth of July before poor William died of the influenza, the summer I was back home with baby Roger while my dear husband was off in the Great War."

She meant World War One, I realized, startled. Her first husband had been English and a flier, and he'd been shot down just before the Armistice. It all seemed centuries ago to me, but not to her. Great-Aunt Alexandra's face shadowed, then brightened.

"Papa did enjoy our life of Washington! Particularly the parts about the card playing and Sally Fairfax, which distressed dear Mama. But Papa thought it all exceedingly amusing, including Mama's distress, I'm afraid. Will you be doing any scenes from the life of Washington this time, Lisa?"

"Just scenes from the life of the Van Zandts, Great-Aunt Alexandra." There was no point in trying to make her remember who I was.

Great-Aunt Alexandra's face lit up. "Oh, then you must have Grandmama's necklace for it!" Her hands went to her throat and began to fumble with the clasp of the heavy diamonds. "Here. Grandpapa bought this for Grandmama when he made his first strike, you know."

"Great-Aunt Alexandra, I can't take that!"

"Oh, yes, you must. Grandpapa gave it to Grandmama done up in a calico handkerchief, and when Grandmama saw it she thought it was a joke he was playing. She was about to toss it in the fire when he stopped her. It's a delightful scene, and you must use it!" Great-Aunt Alexandra thrust the necklace into my hands and closed my fingers over it. "And now I must go find Franz Frederick. We are going to a reception for the Grand Duke, and we must not be late. Goodbye, my dear."

I'd met so many new relatives lately that it took me a minute to remember that Franz Frederick had been her second husband, and he'd only been dead for something like sixty years.

Great-Aunt Alexandra rose, smiling gently, and wandered out onto the porch, calling, "Franz! Franz Frederick! Where are you, dear?" while I sat in the dimness looking after her, my own eyes stinging.

V

Gran's birthday dinner—her *real* birthday dinner—was much like dinner my first night in town. Except that there were a few nonfamily faces there (the Lincoln Center and museum people), and Gran's caftan was apple green, not violet. Great-Aunt Alexandra was in her black lace gown and had wound yards of pearls around her neck in place of the diamond necklace. I wondered if the pearls were real (they looked like mothballs), and when I could get Gran alone for a moment after dinner, I told her about the necklace business.

"It's all right. I'll keep the necklace for you, if you want, till it's time for your picture show. Alexandra's right, the famous necklace should be in it." Gran smiled at me. "I don't want to interfere with your plans, but you should play Grandmother Van Zandt yourself. Have you seen her picture in the family albums? In the necklace and the dress she wore to a party for Jenny Lind—off-shoulder neckline with a lace bertha, and a three-flounced skirt. It's in the attic somewhere. You have the same half smile, when you're growing angry and trying to avoid a confrontation."

Good grief, I thought, flushing. That was all too good a description of my mother. "Great-Aunt Alexandra told me the story about the necklace," I said. Then I stopped, remembering, and swallowed hard. "Gran? She . . . kept expecting Franz Frederick to come in."

Gran nodded. "She gets confused sometimes. Pay no attention to it, please, Laura. We don't want Alexandra to feel sad or worried about it, do we?" She gave me her vague, radiant smile and moved off toward her guests.

The Official Birthday dawned hot. And I do mean dawn—I slept fitfully and awoke with the sky still gray to hear a faint rhythmic humming coming from downstairs. Not Jay again at this hour— I tiptoed down, and there was Gran at the potter's wheel, bent over her work in the shadows in her characteristic pose.

"For heaven's sake, is that jar so important you have to finish it on a day like this?" I asked, half laughing.

"Laura!" Gran looked up, her face luminous. "I hope I didn't wake you. I remembered I'd never wrapped this, and thought I'd better come see—thank you for taking care of it for me."

"It was nothing. Wrapping it up, I mean. The jar's lovely." I went over and stood for a moment, watching the jar grow taller, flare, and then narrow again beneath her sensitive fingers. "It is beautiful, Serena, but on a day as busy as this one do you have to—?" I broke off, turning scarlet. "I'm sorry, I guess I've gotten used to thinking of you that way—"

"As Serena? Why should I mind? It's who I am. I'm not just Gran, or Mother, you know. Even if—" Now it was Gran who broke off, and I knew that she'd been thinking about my mother. Somewhat to my own surprise, I put my arms around her waist and hugged her.

"Anyway," Gran said briskly, "it's not a case of 'have to' . . . well, maybe it is, at that. Only not 'have to finish,' but 'have to do.'" All at once, like a bird in flight, she was off the low stool, lifting the jar and its stand off the potter's wheel and scooping a handful of clay out of a nearby bin. "You come try it!"

"I don't know how."

"You can learn." Gran closed my fingers around the clay, the way Great-Aunt Alexandra had around the necklace. "Just throw it onto the center of the wheel. That's it . . . almost! Now sit down, and move the pedal back and forth with your right foot. That's right." The wheel began turning slowly like a Lazy Susan. "Now, put your hands around it and think about the center of the wheel. Just think *center* and keep your hands steady."

The clay grew into an egg shape, then lurched drunkenly.

I took my foot off the pedal, and the wheel stopped. "I can't."

"Yes, you can. Someday. You're not concentrating now." Gran returned the misshapen clay to the bin and wrapped her jar. "I'd better get back. Your great-aunt is a very light sleeper these days, and she gets flustered if I'm not there when she wakes. Remember, Laura, brunch today is at twelve-thirty. Do try to make Sophie and Jay be there on time."

She said it sweetly, but I'd definitely received my orders.

After Gran left, I took my rehearsal notes and a glass of orange juice out on the front porch. The sky was apricot-colored behind the trees, and birds were singing. After a while Beth wandered over.

"What are you doing out so early?" I demanded.

"I could ask you the same thing." Beth looked over my shoulder at the notes and sketches. "Oh."

"They're *my* reason for not sleeping," I said pointedly. "What's yours?"

Beth shrugged. "It's hot."

"Sure. Except that Wisteria Cottage has all that totally anachronistic but efficient air conditioning. And you wrote that you wanted us to have a chance to talk." I gave her a sideways glance, then looked away. "You wrote something else, too, only you scratched it out."

Beth shrugged again. "You know what it's like when you write letters in the middle of the night. It's almost as bad as writing a diary—oh, look, there's Carl!" she broke off with relief. "I wonder what he's doing out so early."

The surrey, complete with a nosebag for Silver, was rolling cheerfully around the square. Carl stopped at our curb and hauled large cartons out of the back seat. "I've brought some costumes and such for you to look at. I knew if I didn't do it before the sun was up there'd be no way to keep them secret. Your grandmother's an early bird."

I giggled. "I hate to tell you, but she's out already. She left here ten minutes ago, heading back for breakfast with Great-Aunt Alexandra."

We took the cartons inside and Beth made coffee while Carl and I unpacked.

"How are you going to keep Gran from seeing the rehearsal?" Beth returned with the coffee tray, skirting piles of dimities and taffetas as she did so. The rehearsal was taking place in Gran's double parlor at ten A.M.

Carl grinned. "The Pittsburgh newspaper's sending someone over to interview her at the museum. And don't you ever let her know I set that up! They've promised to keep her occupied till noon."

I groaned. Two hours to get the whole show organized! Thank goodness for Aunt Lisa's sketches.

Together, Beth and Carl and I went through the clothing, matching it up with Aunt Lisa's sketches, the sketches Carl had given me earlier, and my list of scenes.

I also had several of the photographs from Gran's albums, which Carl looked at with interest.

"Here's Serena the Third's taffeta ball gown." Carl pulled out the dress Gran had spoken of. It was turquoise watered silk, the color of my eyes, and the flounces were delicate black lace.

Beth caught her breath. "Laura, you have to wear that! It's the right size, too."

"If I don't breathe, you mean," I retorted. "No, thanks. It would fit you better."

"I'm not going to be in the show," Beth said hastily.

"Oh, yes, you are. I need you. I'm not asking you to dance, for Pete's sake, so you don't have to worry about not living up to your professional standards."

Beth's eyes became steely. "You're the one who looks like Serena the Third," she said uncompromisingly, "patronizing smile and all."

Carl stood up. "When the Van Zandt women start fighting, it's time for me to get out of here. I'll have the props you need over at the house by eleven." He stopped in the doorway to give me a long, thoughtful look. "Beth's right, you know. You should be Serena Three."

Beth and Aunt Lisa and I took the clothes across to Gran's house in our cars as soon as we saw Gran being carted off in the surrey to her interview. By now the morning was hot, and so was I. It didn't help that Jay and Sophie and Aunt Rena all straggled in late and decidedly unserious. There was only one direction for the rehearsal to go after that, and it went there. Drastically.

By a quarter to eleven I'd had all that I could take. I grabbed the Chinese gong and mallet off a side table and banged them. Hard.

"Okay!" I shouted as the vibrations died away in the startled silence. "We've got two choices. Either we call this whole thing off right now before we embarrass Gran and ourselves. Or we get to work!"

"She's right, you know." The voice, quiet and matter of fact, came from the far corner of the double parlor, and it was Jay's voice. Amid an astonished stillness he disentangled himself from Sophie and came toward me, absolutely serious, and picked up the calico bag Carl had provided for the diamond necklace. "Let's get the necklace scene fixed up first, shall we?"

Everybody else picked up their cue. We set up the giving-the-necklace scene, then the scene with Aunt Rena as an alluring Serena the First and Uncle Roger as a tall Ben Franklin. By the time Carl arrived, ten minutes late and laden with priceless props, all twelve scenes were what Aunt Lisa called "reasonably roughed in." I'd even, on sudden inspiration, found a scene for Great-Aunt Alexandra. She sat in a mahogany rocker, poignant in shadows, duplicating a photograph of her own mother in old age.

There was a moment of silence when I finished arranging that, and I saw Aunt Rena wiping her eyes.

Saturday rolled on in flower-scented glory. Brunch by the river turned the calendar back to the turn of the century. Afterward Gran insisted that she and Great-Aunt Alexandra take naps—for my great-aunt's sake, I was sure. Everybody else scattered. I went over all the details of the Living Pictures, and bit my nails, and finally wandered over to the workshop, where Carl found me and told me to stop worrying.

"You're not Serena's granddaughter for nothing. Your work will turn out fine."

"Ha," I said, thinking of Sophie. In a lot of senses.

To my surprise, both Sophie and Jay turned up at the next event, afternoon tea, and a chamber music concert in Gran's double parlor, on time and looking absolutely proper. After the concert (Uncle Roger played the flute), we scattered again to dress for dinner. I thought hard, and then I marched across the lawn to Wisteria Cottage and up to Beth's room.

Beth was lying on the bed, intent on a drawing she was making on a large sketch pad. I went in, closing the door behind me, and she didn't even hear me. I tiptoed over, took a look, and exclaimed involuntarily.

"Beth, that's Aunt Rena! And what a great dress you've put her in. I never knew you were an artist!"

Beth slammed the sketch pad shut. "I'm not. This is just fooling around. I like to do caricatures, and design costumes for dances and stuff. Aunt Rena's such a caricature to start with, I wanted to see what she'd look like playing it straight for a change—that's all."

"She'd look a darn sight more like real people, that's for sure." I took the sketch pad out of Beth's hands and had another look. "Honestly, Beth, you're really good. Doesn't Aunt Lisa think so?"

"She doesn't know. And don't you go telling her, or Gran either." Beth's eyes were very bright. "One artist in the family is enough. I do this for fun." There was the slightest emphasis on that word, *fun,* that made me look at her sharply. Beth put the sketch pad carefully away and looked at me gravely. "If you've come to bully me into that darn picture show, don't bother."

"I didn't come to bully. I came to beg. Beth, please, you saw what the scene of Gran when she was young looked like this morning! I put Aunt Rena in it because I didn't trust Sophie, but Aunt Rena's too old, and I don't really trust her either. How do you think Gran's going to feel if Aunt Rena gets the urge to turn on the sex appeal at that point? Aunt Rena won't mind stepping aside; she's doing Serena the First also, and that's lots more fun for her. I need you to do that scene."

"You're the one—"

"—who looks the most like Serena," I finished the sentence for her. "Don't remind me. You already used that line on me, you and Carl, to make me do Serena the Third. I'm not doing both of them. I've got to be backstage riding herd on everybody."

"I could do that."

"No, you can't," I said ruthlessly. "You're not bossy enough. After this morning everybody's decided I'm a class A bitch anyway, so I might as well take advantage of that and crack the whip."

"That's not what they think," Beth said surprisingly. "Everybody had a lot of respect for you. Even Sophie. And Jay. Especially Jay."

There was a very laden silence. I felt myself turning red. Then, to my astonishment, Beth rose, her eyes adult and very gentle. "Don't be embarrassed. If you want to take him away from Sophie, go ahead and do it. He'd be a lot better off."

"I don't—"

"Oh, yes, you do," Beth contradicted. "And you can. Remember what Gran's always saying? 'Think positive.' " All at once she giggled. "I'd positively love to see you walk off with Jay right under Sophie's nose. Somebody's got to jolt her out of how she's been behaving lately."

"Speaking of jolting people out of the ruts they're in—"

"Okay, okay! I'll do the scene for you."

I'd have felt better if Beth hadn't had that Joan-of-Arc-at-the-stake look on her face as she said that.

There wasn't time to tackle the what's-bugging-Beth

issue now. Beth pulled a lovely, ankle-length dress of lace and voile out of her closet, and I ran back across the lawn to the Potter's House to get dressed myself, wishing I'd known in advance that I was going to be here for Gran's birthday. My flowered voile was definitely not going to be up to everybody else's standard.

I went up the steps, and a big Lord & Taylor box was leaning against the door. Carl had scrawled a note across it: UNITED PARCEL DELIVERED THIS AT OFFICE FOR YOU. C.L. I carried the box inside, wondering, and broke the seals. When I lifted the lid, a receipt charged to my parents' account fluttered out and with it a note:

KNOWING SERENA, YOU'RE GOING TO NEED SOME-THING LIKE THIS FOR HER BIG DAY. SORRY I DIDN'T THINK OF THAT BEFORE WE LEFT HOME. HOPE THIS FITS. HAVE FUN. LOVE, DAD.

Beneath the tissue was one of the most gorgeous dresses I had ever seen. It was very plain, but it was peacock-blue chiffon, ankle length, with a low neck front and back, tiny sleeves, and a swirling skirt. And it fit perfectly. Bless Dad, I thought, and bless him for noticing more than I'd thought.

And then, I swear without my conscious intent, the picture of Dad's face in my mind's eye was replaced with one of Jay.

This would never do—heart pounding, I rushed

through a bath, and brushed my hair until it crackled, and put on some turquoise eye shadow, and my silver-hoop earrings. And then the Dress.

When I looked in the mirror, the family resemblance scared me.

Getting into that now won't do, either, I told myself firmly. I jammed my feet into my white sandals and ran downstairs in time to meet Beth and Aunt Lisa on their way to the festivities. Beth exclaimed over the dress, of course, and I saw a startled look of recognition in Aunt Lisa's eyes. But to my profound gratitude, she made no comment.

Dad had known his Serena, all right. Everybody was dressed to the teeth. Even Sophie, for once, was wearing a skirt that skimmed the floor instead of her derriere. And Jay was in a tuxedo that was worlds away from any I'd ever seen at a hometown prom—

Cut that out, I told myself sternly, and tried hard not to look at him through dinner.

After dinner was not so easy, for we were thrown together, getting ready for the Living Picture show. Gran ordered the guests not involved into the library for coffee while Carl, who had shown up to help, arranged chairs in rows in the front parlor and I bullied Jay, who was in a goofing-off mood, into setting up the furniture for the first scene.

"It must be genetic," Jay murmured when I yelped for the third time for him to watch out for breakables.

"What?" I snapped automatically, diving for a tottering porcelain vase.

"The bossiness. And the beauty. Are you sure your name's Laura? That was definitely Aunt Serena's voice I heard you use." I started, setting the table the vase was on rocking again. This time it was Jay who caught it.

"Hey, hey, calm down. It'll be all right on the night, as the backstage saying goes." Jay's fingers rested on my wrist to feel my pulse, then brushed a wisp of hair out of my eyes. "Same hair, too, according to my Gran. But you're definitely lovelier."

"Save that line for Sophie," I said shortly.

"No, I mean it—hey, wait! I'm sorry if I've made you mad. It was meant as a compliment—" Jay's voice, definitely no longer teasing, came after me as I rushed away.

I had to get into Serena the Third's dress at once, because I'd have to be "in the wings" to make sure the earlier scenes went smoothly.

Aunt Lisa helped me into the corset and crinolines and hooked up the rustling taffeta. And she insisted on doing my hair. "Now look," she said at last, ushering me before the pier glass mirror of the downstairs bedroom.

The family auburn hair gleamed like satin, framing a heart-shaped, high-cheekboned face. The black lace bertha fell softly off my shoulders. I couldn't breathe.

At that moment, Jay's face showed in the mirror behind our shoulders. I blotted out everything but the admiration in his eyes.

Perhaps fortunately, we didn't get a chance to speak. Distantly, Liu was ringing the gong. Aunt Lisa slipped out. From beyond the drawn portieres that separated the two parlors, I heard the rustle of the audience settling down. I heard paper rustling—Carl had had programs copied. Then I heard Aunt Lisa at the piano.

From the moment the portieres opened that first time, I knew we were breathing the heady air of success. The audience response rolled toward us in warm waves; even behind the scenes I could feel it. Laughter came at all the right times, especially at the demure expression on Aunt Rena's face. Then it was time for Jay and me—

I took the pose Aunt Lisa had sketched, my downstage hand just lifting the diamond necklace from the calico kerchief, my upstage hand in astonishment at my lips. Jay, his frock coat dashing and his eyes wicked, held the kerchief steady. The portieres opened.

I heard a faint gasp, and I knew it came from Gran. Otherwise there was a silence. Then applause. It registered on me vaguely that there was a portrait of Serena the Third in the library. The audience must have just been looking at it.

The portieres closed. The music started. The show went on. Jay had a fast costume change, because he was due to appear again as Grandfather Harris, this time with Beth.

I couldn't remember too much about the show, because I had too much on my mind. I did notice, with relief, that Beth got through her scene all right and that Sophie had behaved okay. I noticed the rush of emotion in the room, and the stillness, when Great-Aunt Alexandra sat in her rocker, being Great-Grandmother. I noticed the applause at the end.

We hadn't done anything about curtain calls, so the portieres swished shut and stayed shut. Aunt Lisa came over and hugged me. Then Sophie, who had promptly ducked out front to collect audience reaction, appeared.

"Hey, Laura! You and Jay have to do your scene again. Special command from the Queen."

Jay and I took our places. We heard Aunt Lisa stepping out front and demanding, laughingly, "Silence, everyone!" She seated herself at the piano and began to play one of Jenny Lind's favorite songs. Carl was working the curtains. He looked at me, gave me a wink and a grin, and swept them open.

For half a minute Jay and I stood there, maintaining our careful pose to delighted murmurs and a ripple of applause. Then, without warning, Jay changed the script.

He pulled the diamond necklace back from my fingers, and he came around behind me and clasped it around my neck. And then, as my heart was pounding, he deliberately put one hand on my shoulder and the other at my waist, and turned me around and kissed me. Hard.

He held the kiss as if it were part of the living picture, as the applause and laughter grew. He held me because he was bending me half backward and without his support I would have fallen. Because of the pose and something more.

When the curtains closed and he released me, he gave me a salute and a meaningful look, half serious, half laughing. And, blessedly, walked off, leaving me all too close to a Victorian faint.

Mother'd been afraid to have me come to this re-union. Mother'd been too darn right. Things had changed. I'd changed. For starters, I'd fallen in love with my cousin Jay Tremaine. And if, as Tina Turner sang, there was a question as to what love had to do with it, that was something I didn't want to think about right now.

VI

Serena Van Zandt Harris
requests the pleasure of your company
at the dedication of
Vredezucht
the Van Zandt Family Homestead Museum Village

PROGRAM
Friday, July the First
Dinner at the Nathaniel Van Zandt House, 8 p.m.

Saturday, July the Second
Welcome, the Village Green, 11 a.m.
Luncheon on the Opera House Terrace, 12 noon
Tour of the Village, 2:30 p.m.
Dedication Ceremonies, the Village Green, 5 p.m.
Reception at the Crafts Museum,
immediately following
Dinner at the Monongahela House, 7 p.m.

Concert and Evening Entertainment,
the Opera House, 8:30 p.m.

Sunday, July the Third
Church Service, 11 a.m.
Brunch at the Monongahela House, 12:30 p.m.
Chamber Music Concert at the Opera House, 4 p.m.
River Picnic commencing on the Terrace, 6 p.m.

Monday, July the Fourth
Flag-raising, the Village Green, 9:30 a.m.
Independence Day Parade commencing at 10 a.m.
Van Zandt Family Fourth of July Picnic
on the lawns of the Nathaniel Van Zandt House
commencing at 3 p.m.
Band Concert on the Village Green, 7:30 p.m.
Fireworks Display commencing at dusk

Serena had her own carefully worked out schedule for what Sophie took to calling Van Zandt Rattle the Skeletons Week. For us ordinary mortals, all kinds of private agendas were operating beneath the surface.

Sophie was right. Skeletons were definitely rattling.

Sophie arrived to rattle mine before I was even awake the morning following the Living Pictures. She yanked the sheet off me, settled herself at the foot of the bed, and announced, "I don't believe this. I thought you were one of those good little girls who bounces up

81

bright and early Sunday morning to go to church."

"I thought you were one of those who thinks early morning means one P.M.," I groaned.

"Wrong. I'm a good girl, I am," Sophie retorted, lapsing into Cockney. "I do know when to behave myself, contrary to what some people think. I'm even going to church with the rest of you."

I did a double-take. Sophie was wearing a white cotton dress so demure it covered her from throat to knees, a white sailor hat, and even gloves, so help me. "I'm impressed," I said and meant it. Then I looked at the clock. "It's not church that brings you here at eight A.M. What gives?"

"That's what I'd like to know, luv." Sophie took out a pack of cigarettes, lit up, and blew smoke at the ceiling. "Interesting encore to the picture show last night. Had you and Jay been rehearsing?"

I turned scarlet. "Of course not. Hey!" Sophie had tossed the burned-out match carelessly onto the hooked rug. "Pick that up. Please."

"My, my, we are touchy this morning, aren't we?" Sophie blew smoke again, not stirring. I scrambled out of bed, got the match, and took it to the bathroom, glad of the excuse. I splashed water on my face and came back with all the dignity that I could muster.

"You didn't have to bother with that," Sophie said knowingly. "This is just me, toots. You can level. Are you falling for that gorgeous cousin of ours, or have you just got the hots for him? Or are you just keeping in practice?"

The best defense was a good offense, Mother always said. "Why? Is he your private property?" I demanded.

"I don't think Jay's the type to be anybody's private property," Sophie said. "Not that I am, either. Just a word to the wise between cousins. Watch your step. You're not in his league, and you could get hurt."

"How do you know what league I'm in?"

"Do *you* know?" Sophie's voice was mocking, but it had serious undertones. And it was hitting too close for comfort.

"You smoke too much," I said, banging bureau drawers as she stubbed out the old cigarette on the hearth and lit another.

"Bloody truth, you *do* sound like the Queen." Sophie slid to her feet. "What I get for trying to do you a favor, I suppose. Ta for now. I wish Aunt Kay were here."

At that moment, so did I.

Sunday, on the surface at least, was calm. We all went to church together. We went over to the Monongahela House for brunch. In the afternoon I went for a walk, on the back streets, hoping to avoid all my near and dear. When a car horn tooted, I jumped.

It wasn't a relative, it was Carl, leaning out of his own blue Honda. "I'm doing an airport run. Want to come for the ride? I promise not to say one word about events, recent or future." So I climbed in beside him and we drove a couple of the stragglers to the Pittsburgh airport. Afterward Carl bought me supper at Houlihan's in the Station Square mall, and true to his promise we didn't say a word about anything at Vredezucht.

I didn't even think about Jay till I was home in bed.

That was Sunday. On Monday I again woke to hear the potter's wheel turning. This time I knew what to expect, or thought I did. I pulled on a robe, went down, and said, "Hi, Gran," and put on the coffeepot.

And Gran, not even looking up, said, "I want the Living Pictures repeated at the Opera House next Saturday evening."

I almost dropped the coffeepot in shock. "You *what?*"

"You heard me," Gran said matter-of-factly. "You did an excellent job, and I want to share the results with our weekend guests."

"Your guests, you mean." I took a deep breath. "Gran, you've got a couple of hundred people coming. You're giving them a concert by professional musicians. We can't just . . . stick in a little amateur performance—"

"I don't expect it to be amateur," Gran said calmly. "You can add a few more scenes to make the program longer. Plan on a half hour to three-quarters of an hour." She turned back to her wheel as if the matter were all settled.

"Why are you telling me? Why not Carl, or Jay— the pictures were his idea."

"They may have been his idea originally, but it was you who took the reins when that was needed. You are family. Carl will help, of course. Oh, and tell Beth I certainly expect her to dance. There's been enough of this nonsense of her effacing herself." Gran stopped pedaling, gave her jar a long scrutiny before rewrapping it, and left without coffee but with one of those radiant smiles.

"Why are you surprised?" Beth asked when I told her about Gran's visit later. "She's proud of what you pulled off the other night, and you should be, too. Getting just about our whole family onstage together, not speaking, and no blood shed?"

"It wasn't onstage. It was in Gran's living room."

"Some living room. The Opera House won't be that much different. At least you'll have backstage space," Beth pointed out.

"What do you mean, *me*? You're in this, too. Gran expects you to dance. Command performance." I caught at Beth's arm as she turned away. "Quit pulling the disappearing act and listen to me. I promise I'll keep Gran and Aunt Lisa off your case this week. But the only way I'll be able to is if you bite the bullet and *dance*. You must know some routine you can get away with! Let me swear you'll do that, and I swear I'll make them stay away from you. I'll tell them your artistic temperament needs a rest, or something."

To my relief, after several minutes Beth managed half a smile. "Okay," she said soberly. "Okay. One dance. No encores." She gave me a look from beneath lowered lashes. "We'll leave the encores to you and Jay."

"Now *you* cut it out!"

That was Monday. On Tuesday a letter arrived for me from Mother.

Laura, luv—London's exciting; this job is even more so. Fed the loons and pelicans in St. James Park on Sunday morning and met the most fascinating man—reporter for one of the London scandal sheets—shame on him! But he really is a serious journalist beneath the surface—is arranging for me to meet all sorts of useful people. Hear you went to the Queen's birthday party after all. Watch your step, sweetie. I know you find Serena fascinating, but she'll cannibalize you if you don't watch out. Talk to Lisa if you have unanswered questions. Will write when I can, but I'm terribly busy. Going up to the Midlands tomorrow doing field research with one of my sources—university towns later. I feel a book jelling in my head! At last, at last. . . ! 'Bye for now, sweetie—behave yourself and have fun in equal measure. . . .

The letter worried me, though there was nothing in it I could put my finger on. At least Mom didn't explode over my being here, I thought. But that in itself was odd, wasn't it?

In the late afternoon I called Dad, but couldn't reach him, and it was nearly eleven P.M. when he returned my call. "Laura? Are you all right?"

"Sure I'm all right. Just feeling kind of homesick, I guess. I heard from Mom. Have you?"

"What did she say?"

"Having a great time, book going well. You know. The usual Mom-in-the-throes-of-creation. I'll show you when you get here. You are coming for the Fourth, aren't you?"

"I'm definitely planning on it. But I'm still not sure exactly when my work in Philadelphia will be finished," Dad replied. "I may have to leave Wisconsin again as soon as we get back there."

"We can cross that bridge when we get to it," I said blithely. But after I put the receiver down, I felt uneasy.

I was beginning to get the whim-whams about repeating the Living Picture show as part of Gran's Glorious Fourth, anyway. Doing the tableaux in Gran's drawing room had been one thing. Doing them on the stage of the Opera House, with a lot of professional performers around, was another.

I took a deep breath and started phoning around that there'd be three rehearsals—Wednesday, Thursday, and Friday, with nobody excused. Predictably I heard grumbles. I spent Wednesday morning at the

Opera House, with Aunt Lisa and Carl, planning scene changes and lighting and things like that.

Wednesday afternoon we had a run-through. Only it turned out to be practically a whole restaging. The stage was a lot bigger than Gran's drawing room. More furniture and other props were needed. Poses had to be changed. Stage lights had to be focused. People got cranky about having to stand motionless in place while this was done. The electrician who had to move the lights was annoyed about the whole darn project.

"I've done this once already, focusing lights for the professionals," he grumbled. "Why can't you people just stand in the same pools of light I set up for them?"

"Because it won't work," I said shortly. But I did rearrange a couple of scenes to eliminate the need for a few lighting instruments. Of course, that didn't please everybody, either.

After rehearsal, Jay pulled me aside. "Let's go swimming."

"Later. If I can. I should stay in here and see what I can do to make things go smoother at the next rehearsal." Involuntarily I sighed.

"Laura, look at me," Jay said sternly. "*You* weren't the one who made this rehearsal rough. And there's no reason you should do your whole job over just because other people don't feel like doing theirs." I blinked, and Jay's voice softened. "I know you don't like to throw your weight around—"

"I don't have any to throw."

"Yes, you do, whether you realize it or not. I just want to say I respect you for not pulling rank. But if you let people walk all over you without standing up for yourself, you're giving away your right to be respected. And I don't mean as Serena's granddaughter. I mean as Laura Blair. Now how about that swim? The river's great!"

"Okay," I said recklessly. "Okay!"

We swam for half an hour and then flopped in the sun on the grassy bank. By then I was out of breath, for a lot of reasons. I glanced over at Jay, then away, and wondered what I'd do if he tried to kiss me.

He didn't. He propped himself up on one elbow, looked at me, and said, "Now tell Uncle Jay what's wrong."

"What do you mean?"

"You know the answer to that one, not me. Ever since Saturday you've been avoiding me. Okay, so maybe I know the reason for that," he said quickly as I blushed. "We'll let it ride for now. Ever since Tuesday morning you've been a cross between Aunt Serena jet-propelled and Aunt Rena skating on thin ice without anything to hold onto."

The description was so accurate it took my breath away. So did his next words. "Does it have anything to do with Uncle Ken and Aunt Kay?"

"What—made you think of that?"

"I know families. I know Sophie and Aunt Rena. Just adding two and two," Jay said and tactfully looked away as I wiped my eyes.

"It isn't anything," I said at last. "I'm just . . . missing my folks, I guess. I don't know when Mom's coming home, and—wait a minute. How do you know so much about families? Didn't your parents die when you were young?"

"Sure, and before that I didn't see them too much. But a fellow knows."

We let the silence settle.

"Jay?" I said tentatively. "How did you feel about it? Not seeing your parents, I mean. Not having a traditional family unit. How did you get used to it?"

Jay shrugged. "I just don't let myself need people all that much. I learned that a long time ago."

"It sounds lonely."

Jay didn't answer.

After a while we swam again and acted silly, and Jay was gentle with me, protective, but he didn't kiss me. He's seeing me as a kid sister, I thought, not sure whether I was disappointed or relieved.

That swim by the river was about the only breather either of us got all week. Putting together the Living Pictures for Gran's birthday had been a picnic compared to the pressures involved in the repeat performance. I needed more props and costumes. I needed more people. Carl, bless him, managed to locate both, drafting some of the more prominent townspeople and staff members. They seemed flattered to be asked. A lot of them called me "Miss Blair," and at first that made me feel uncomfortable. Then I realized that the formality made it easier for me to have control.

I had to have control, not because I was Serena's granddaughter, but because I was responsible for the end result, and that was the only way to make sure the result would be right.

"The single-eye view," Aunt Lisa called it, and explained: "The difference between an amateur and a professional performance is usually that with amateurs everybody has his own view of how the show should be. Professionals know that while a show needs everybody's talents, there has to be one angle of vision. Otherwise there's no perspective. There has to be just one camera lens." She laughed. "Listen to me preaching a sermon! But that's one of the things I was taught in art school, and Beth in ballet. Mother would say it's all in the Bible. Twelfth Corinthians. Everybody has unique talents, and each talent has a different place. And yours for now, sweetie, is in the director's seat. So don't be afraid to use it!"

Carl had a different metaphor. "See those swans on the river? They just glide along, but underwater their feet are paddling like mad. That's the way to get results. No *sturm und drang*."

"What's that mean?"

"*Storm and Stress,* the title of a nineteenth-century German play about the American Revolution, and the way most amateurs louse things up. Being like a swan is your grandmother's secret."

Thursday ran into Friday, and all the pieces of Gran's Glorious Fourth began to fit together. I held a rehearsal Friday afternoon, and I cracked the whip, and things did go well, if I do say so. By dinnertime many of Gran's official guests had arrived and were stowed away at various restored houses or the Monongahela House. Gran's dinner party was very grand. We cousins faded into the woodwork and were glad to do so.

On Saturday morning the official opening ceremonies of the village got under way. When we were having lunch on the Opera House terrace, Carl came to find me. "There's a telephone call for you in my office. It's your father."

Dad should have been on the plane by now. I ran inside and picked up the phone apprehensively. *"Dad?"*

"Whoa there, sweetheart! Nothing's wrong. Except that I'm afraid I'm not going to be able to join you for the weekend after all."

"Dad, what happened?"

"Work. I told you what it's been like here, remember?" Work over Fourth of July weekend? my mind wondered. "Have you heard anything from your mother?"

"Not since that one letter. Why? Have you?"

Dad laughed. "You know your mother! If she's

psyched into her new project, she'll be tearing around too wound up to write. Laura, I am sorry about this weekend. Give your grandmother my love. I'll see you both as soon as it's possible. And remember, you can call me any time you want. I have to go now. Someone's waiting."

It was a very equivocal conversation.

I wandered back to the luncheon. Jay saw my expression and asked me what was wrong, and I told him. He repeated his advice about not needing people too much. Beth asked, too, and when I told her she didn't say anything, just hugged me.

Saturday wound on through the tour, the dedication ceremonies, the reception. After that came dinner at the Monongahela House. I wore Dad's peacock dress and ate little. Afterward everybody went to the Opera House. The entertainment included some famous people and was pretty special, but by halfway through it I was jumping out of my skin. I sneaked out and went backstage to change into my Serena the Third costume.

Pretty soon everyone else came drifting back, too. The air became heady with excitement and muted laughter.

"Where's Jay?" I asked suddenly.

All at once, beneath the excitement, there was a stillness. It was coming from Beth and Sophie, and I stared. "Didn't you tell her?" Sophie demanded, and Bath, her face whitening, shook her head.

"I thought you were going to."

"Tell me what?" I demanded. I went over and grabbed Sophie.

"Jay's gone," Sophie said.

"What do you mean, gone?"

"Just that," Sophie said, very busily fixing her hair before a mirror. "He's cut out. Some friend of his showed up in a new Porsche, just as we were coming into the Opera House. He wanted Jay to go to New York with him to see the tall ships in the Harbor Festival, and Jay did."

"Just like that?"

"Just like that," Sophie said. "Guys are like that. Don't tell me you didn't know."

"But the Living Pictures—"

"I tried to talk him out of it," Beth said unhappily. "But he wouldn't listen. He just laughed and said you'd think of something, and that he'd told you not to count on people. Laura, where are you going?"

I didn't have time to answer. Jay had said I'd think of something? Then I darn well would. *I* wasn't going to be the one to let Gran down. I pushed past people till I reached Carl, in jeans and sports shirt, by the lighting board.

"Something's happened. Jay's not here. Will you do his scenes?"

Carl reacted as quickly as I. He headed straight to the men's dressing room to change.

So it was Carl who stood motionless with me in the

diamond necklace scene, and this time there was no picture come to life, and no kissing. There was the same, even louder, applause, the same wave of warm affection rolling across the footlights. And at the laughing cries of "Author! Director!" I came out and curtsied. At the refreshment hour that followed in the ballroom, I smiled, and accepted compliments and returned them. But inside I felt cold.

I was "letting things roll off me." I was "not letting myself need people," as Jay had advised. It was a lesson I'd never expected or wanted to have to learn. I felt like somebody'd died.

VII

Journal—Saturday, July 2

Mother, why aren't you here? I need you.

Talk to Aunt Lisa, Dad says. I suppose I could. I suppose I could talk to Gran, but I can't see myself telling her that her grandnephew (or whatever he is) turned me on and then without a second thought walked out on me and her.

Why the hell does Mother have to be Taking Her Writing Seriously this one time when I need her most?

At least she's got a contract with a national publisher for these English articles, I think. She wouldn't break up the family for the summer and go tearing across the Atlantic without one—I keep telling myself.

Unless she was just trying to get away. From Serena. Or something.

We learned something in psych class this year about a fight/flight syndrome. Boy, have I been learning about that lately.

Don't think about all that. Jay said I shouldn't let people *matter so much to me, and maybe he's right. (Darn, there I am thinking about him again!) Think about something nice, like how Beth really, honestly is going to dance for Gran, and how everybody loved the Living Pictures. Some magazine took pictures, including one of me as Serena Three (with Carl, not *@#$%). They're going to run it as part of their coverage of the Museum Village opening.*

So far nobody's written about the effect a Living Legend has on her family. I hate to think of Mother doing that someday, if she ever gets around to writing books instead of just talking about doing so.

Maybe she really will, now that she's all psyched up about this English project. I don't mean I really believe she'd write one of those My Mother the Witch *books. Maybe she would, if she got into such a tailspin that she didn't think through what she was doing.*

Maybe I don't know my mother as well as I thought I did. Not anymore.

Mother. What do I know about my mother? There's no Serena in her name, but her middle name's Van Zandt, and she's spent most of her thirty-nine—nearly forty—years trying to live it down. The Katherine is for Katherine Parr, Henry the Eighth's last wife, who according to Serena had a good slice of beauty, wit, and wisdom, too.

My mother the emancipated woman thinks being told you have beauty, wit, and wisdom is a chauvinist pig/sexist putdown. The fact that she's all those things—when she lets herself be them—is something she chooses to ignore. She ignores the great bone structure she inherited from Gran, and hides curves I could die for under layers of bag-lady clothing.

Dad hates the way she dresses. He never says so, but I know he has to. He always looks so conservative, and neat, and he keeps giving her gorgeous lacy sleepwear, and silk blouses, and stuff like that. And Mom puts it in her bureau drawer and wears his old flannel pajamas, and jeans she had in college with heaven knows what on top.

I've never told anybody this before: Once, when she was writing that "Supermom" column—that was when I was in junior high—she was asked to come speak on a Visiting Writers Day at our school. It was a special program, run by a committee of the kids, the head of the English department, and the school librarian. Students were introducing all the speakers, and escorting them around from class to class. The student body voted to make it a dress-up day. I mean the boys even wore jackets and ties. And Mother showed up in those jeans, with an old jumper I'd discarded as too childish on top of it as a tunic, and under the jumper one of Dad's silk gift blouses, with a turtleneck T-shirt of his beneath it. And a cape, and a slouch hat.

I guess she thought she looked romantically bohemian. I never told her what I heard the kids saying behind her back.

I wonder if she dressed like that when Dad first met her. I wonder what they saw in each other then. Chemistry? Did they think that was enough?

I wonder if there's any chemistry left.

Sunday, the third of July. Beautiful Sunday morning, a cross between Norman Rockwell and Currier & Ives. The roses were in bloom. Even the reporters trailing around after Gran and company looked Sunday solemn, and there I was wondering whether Jay was coming back. I didn't know whom I was more furious with, him or myself.

He didn't show up.

"That's Jay. Hey, that's the family," Sophie said when she saw my face. "One half's so conscientious it hurts, and the other half reacts in the opposite direction. Look at my mother. Look at yours."

"Look at yourself," I said pointedly.

Sophie raised her eyebrows. "So our meek little mouse has got claws after all."

"And don't you dare call me a mouse!"

Gran cornered me in the ladies' room at the Monongahela House during brunch, and asked me point-blank about Jay's disappearance. I told her the truth flat out. Gran didn't say anything, just pressed her lips together; and at that point somebody else came in, so I was off the hook.

After brunch I ran back to the Potter's House and showered, and made it to the Opera House with only minutes to spare before the concert. A string quartet that had also played the night before was going to do some Mozart, and after Beth's dancing, would return with Schubert. Beth was dancing to Bach, with Aunt Lisa at the piano. It was a concert of mostly sacred music, in deference to its being Sunday afternoon, and Beth was doing something that Gran called sacred dance.

As the quartet warmed the audience up, I slipped backstage in search of Beth. She, too, was warming up in an empty soundproofed rehearsal room, with her tape recorder turned on low. The door of the room had a glass pane in it, and I stood on the outside for a moment, watching Beth without her knowing it.

Beth was wearing a pale gray leotard, with her hair sleeked up in an austere dancer's knot. I'd never realized before that she was so beautiful—or so thin. Her face was exalted, as though she were seeing beyond the stars. She traced her beautiful turns, dipped and swayed, lifted her arms toward the sky or bowed her head in a line reminiscent of Gran at the potter's wheel, and something caught in my throat. So this was what Gran meant by dance being sacred.

I crept inside, closing the door cautiously behind me. Beth didn't even know. She was in a trance; she had the look Mother gets when her writing's really coming, the look that Aunt Lisa gets when she's painting. I sat down on the edge of a chair, and for the first time in days my heart grew quiet.

And then it lurched, for Beth lurched, as though

she'd lost her balance. She caught herself against the chair she'd been using as a barre and stood there for a minute, breathing hard, as I ran over.

"Beth! Are you okay?"

Beth stared at me for a minute without focusing. Then she shook her head with a little start. "How long have you been here?" she demanded.

"Just a few minutes. It was beautiful, so I watched. I didn't want to disturb you. You haven't answered my question."

"I'm fine." Beth's chin came up. "I probably just got too much resin on my shoe. Laura, go on out front, and don't say anything about this to anybody. Promise!" Her fingers were clutching my sleeves so tightly that her knuckles showed white.

I did what she asked because I didn't want to upset her by refusing.

The quartet bowed its way through the Mozart and took bows, and the curtains closed so the stage could be cleared. Then the curtains opened again, and Beth was up there dancing.

Other than just now backstage and that day in the woods, this was the first time I'd seen Beth dance since Mom and Dad and I had seen her in the chorus of a dancing school production of *The Nutcracker* when she was ten. Almost immediately the whole auditorium grew silent, a live and throbbing silence. I knew what it meant. Gran's guests had sat back, prepared to be kind to the little amateur relative, and they'd been knocked out of their VIP socks. I knew Beth was a real dancer, like Gran and Aunt Lisa had always said, and I knew it not because of other people's stillness but because of what was happening in my chest and head and stomach. I honestly forgot it was my own cousin up there.

And then I remembered, fast, because the same thing happened that had happened in the rehearsal room, only worse. Beth lurched, and wavered, but recovered and picked the music up on the next beat. She launched into a series of spins, only she didn't make them. At the end of the third she toppled over like a broken doll.

Before the collective gasp was over, before the curtains swept shut, I was squeezing over the knees of the VIPs beside me, running up the aisle, running outside and around the building because it was the fastest way to reach the backstage area with all those other people clogging up the aisles.

I made it onstage only about a minute after Aunt Lisa did, and I reached Beth first because Aunt Lisa was wearing five-inch heels. She lay so still, scarcely breathing, and there were purplish smudges like bruises beneath her closed eyes.

"Don't move her!" Carl called sharply as I dropped down beside her, so I only stroked her hair. Then Aunt Lisa was there, and Gran, and a stout elderly man who was a doctor. Things happened fast. The doctor felt Beth's pulse, and Beth's eyelids fluttered, and then, following instructions, Carl carried her to an old sofa in the wings. Being Beth, or maybe I should say being a Van Zandt, Beth was insisting she was fine *now,* she'd just been too nervous to eat any lunch, and would everybody please leave her alone. The doctor, not to mention Aunt Lisa and Gran, were making noises about a hospital.

Finally a compromise was reached. Carl drove Beth and Aunt Lisa and me back to Wisteria Cottage, and he carried her upstairs. Beth put herself to bed, on condition that Aunt Lisa would go back to the Opera House for the rest of the scheduled events and that I could stay to babysit, provided I stayed downstairs.

"You make me nervous hovering," Beth said bluntly.

So I obeyed, but as soon as Carl and Aunt Lisa had vanished around the green, I broke the rules. I marched upstairs to where Beth was picking at the sandwich Aunt Lisa'd made her, sat down on the bed, and demanded, "Okay, what the hell is going on?"

"Nothing's going on," Beth said stubbornly.

"Don't give me that. You wrote me a cryptic letter, you've been trailing around looking like the wrath of God—"

"Thanks a whole heap."

"Oh, you look gorgeous, too," I went on ruthlessly, "but you know what I mean. You shut everybody out, you didn't want to perform, and now first you almost pass out, and then you do pass out in full view of a couple of hundred people. Do you really think I'm so dumb I don't know something's wrong?"

Beth's chin came up. "Look who's talking!"

"Don't change the subject. We're talking about you right now."

Beth pushed herself up in bed, her eyes enormous. "If anybody's getting me upset, it's you. You made me dance. I told you I didn't want to. No, I didn't think this would happen!" she added hastily. "But you get me so upset. All of you!" She made a violent gesture. "The last thing I need right now is you coming on as strong as Gran! I can feel myself starting to hyperventilate, and I'll be darned if I want to faint again, so either you get the heck out of this room, or *I'm* getting out of it."

I went because I didn't know what else to do.

An hour later Sophie appeared, bringing a basket of goodies from the river picnic. "Was I glad of the excuse to escape!" she exclaimed, setting the food out along the edge of Beth's four-poster bed. "Six hours of being a proper lady is more than I can manage!" She kicked off her shoes and draped herself sideways over an armchair, and entertained Beth and me with raunchy stories about the British heavy metal scene until Aunt Lisa came home. By that time both Beth and Aunt Lisa had been pretty well defused.

Monday was the Fourth of July, a real old-fashioned Fourth of July, which was not as much a novelty to me as to the others, because I'd grown up in Middle America. Beth and Sophie and I watched the festivities from the Wisteria Cottage porch, Beth under doctor's orders, me to be with her, and Sophie so she needn't be proper for Gran's public. Sophie didn't know a darn thing about American history or holidays, and her attitude was to say the least irreverent, so we all had a lot of fun. Afterward, Carl picked us up in the surrey and trundled us around to Gran's for the family picnic. This too was traditional—fried chicken, baked ham, corn on the cob, potato salad and cole slaw in cut crystal bowls, a very familiar teetotal punch, strawberry short-cake, and the same raspberry pudding Mother makes. I'd never known how much of my own immediate family's celebrations had been patterned on Mother's growing up.

Mother. It felt funny, not having Mom and Dad around for the holiday, but I didn't say so.

As the late sunlight began to gray, a band dressed in gold-trimmed red uniforms began to assemble in the gazebo bandstand on the green. I recognized the doctor with a clarinet and one of the waiters from the Monongahela House with a tuba.

"The band's Gran's doing, too," Beth said. "I heard about it the day we came. Dr. Scott told Gran a lot of his local patients used to play in the high school band when they were kids, so Gran recruited them. She recruited the high school band, too, and a couple of guys who play for Duquesne University."

"I've noticed," Sophie said, eyeing some gorgeous hulks.

She eyed them to such good purpose that after the concert they ambled over to introduce themselves, and others followed, and we ended up having quite a fireworks-watching party on the Wisteria Cottage steps. Afterward we transferred to the Potter's House because somewhere along the line in the past two days I'd made a couple of cakes. Maybe in the hope that Dad and Jay would show up after all, but I wasn't letting myself think about that.

It was, all in all, a lovely day—so lovely that, in a rush of family feeling as I went to bed, I reached for the telephone and started to call Mom. Then I realized that it would be four A.M. in London and put the phone down again.

A lot of Gran's guests, the ones who were wage slaves, left on a late plane from Pittsburgh Monday night. Everybody else except family left early Tuesday. The Serena Van Zandt gala was over.

I called Dad's hotel in Philadelphia while I was eating breakfast Tuesday morning, but the switchboard said he'd left word he was not to be disturbed. Yes, they'd take a message. No, they didn't know when he was planning to check out. So I still didn't know when we'd be going back to Elm Grove, Wisconsin. I decided to go check out how Beth was doing, but she'd gone out, too, which had left Aunt Lisa in a state of baffled dismay.

"Would you believe I got up at seven o'clock and she'd already vanished? No note, no nothing. As soon as I finish this cup of coffee, I'm going out in the car to look for her," Aunt Lisa said with determination.

"I don't think you have to worry," I said, crossing my fingers. "She just needs a little room. At least she didn't act at all like she was sick yesterday. It was probably just the heat."

"Heat, or overdoing the practice sessions, which I doubt, or just plain not eating," Aunt Lisa said grimly. "I know, I know, I'm being a mother hen. You look for her, will you?"

So I did, in all the predictable places, but I didn't find her.

When I got back to the Potter's House, Aunt Lisa's car was gone, and there was a letter from Mother in the mailbox. I took it upstairs to read while I changed into my bathing suit.

Mother's handwriting was more than usually haphazard. Why the dickens doesn't she typewrite her letters? I remember thinking. She carts that portable everywhere with her, and then she writes these scrawls.

"My dear darling Laura," the letter began. "I have something very serious to tell you, and please try to understand—"

And I stood there in my bra and jeans, trying to

decipher the slapdash ball-point pen marks that sprawled across both sides of the translucent airmail paper. And something cold and hard like a frozen snowball slammed into my stomach, and up into my ribcage, and grew and grew. I sat down hard on the edge of the bed, gasping and bent double.

Then my shaking hand clenched into a fist, clenching the paper into a ball and flinging it across the room. My last clear thought was: *I've never felt so sick in all my life.* And then I felt nothing.

VIII

 Quotes to Remember:

OBERON: *Ill met by moonlight, proud Titania.*

TITANIA: *What, jealous Oberon! Fairies, skip hence:*
I have foresworn his bed and company . . .
And this same progeny of evils comes
From our debate, from our dissension;
We are their parents and original.

OBERON: *Do you amend it then; it lies in you.*

I may have cried out. I don't know. I heard a sound, somewhere near, like a dying cat. I heard the blood pounding in my ears. Nothing was real but the pain in my chest, growing like a starburst.

Then there were voices, there were feet pounding on the stair. Sophie's voice calling, "She's not here!"

Then Beth's, "Yes, she is!" Beth's arms going around me. Beth's voice, taut with fright, demanding, "Laura! What happened? What's wrong?"

My teeth were rattling so hard I couldn't answer. I was shivering so hard that my arms, clutched across my chest, couldn't stop the shaking. I shook my head, violently, and finally I was able to get a word out. *"No!"*

"No what? *Laura!*"

Sophie was there now, too. I could smell her musk perfume. I could feel the bones of Beth's ribs as she cradled my face against her chest.

"I'm all right—just let me alone," I gasped.

"Where've I heard that before?" Beth asked quietly. She was rocking me in her arms as Sophie knelt beside us. Beth's gentleness and the rocking helped. I drew a breath and straightened.

"I'm okay now."

"The hell you are," Sophie said bluntly. "We heard you clear next door, and you scared us silly. What was it? Hey, you can tell us. We're family."

"Don't use that word!"

"Oh," Beth said comprehensively and held me again because the shudder was returning.

Sophie went away and returned with a cup of tea as black as ink. "You won't like it, but drink it anyway. It helps. I know."

The cup was warm in my hands. I forced a grin. "How do you know about coping with hysterics?"

"With my mother, and all the boarding schools I've been to, you should ask that?" Sophie's tone was flippant, but her eyes were sober. "Look, kid, wherever you are, I bet anything I've been there. I know hysterics, and I know crashing from highs. And I know shock trauma, 'cause I was in a car crash once. Omitting the blood, that's what you look like now."

"Like you said, there's no blood shed!" I strove to copy Sophie's joking tone. "Look, guys, I appreciate the solicitude . . . but it's not needed. Something just . . . frightened me—"

My voice wasn't cooperating with me anymore. Neither were my eyelids, which no longer held back the tears. I buried my face against Beth's T-shirt, and when Beth whispered, "What was it, Laura? You've got to tell us," I shook my head.

"There's got to be some clue around here," Sophie said, and then, "Oh."

I heard the rustle of paper and knew what it was. I wrenched myself free of Beth's restraining arms. It was too late. Sophie was already flattening Mother's letter out on the floor. When I grabbed for it, she jerked away.

"Sophie, don't—please—"

Sophie ignored me. She took the letter to the window and began to read to herself. "Ohh," I heard her say. And then she read aloud the awful words I'd tried not to recognize, tried to blot from my mind.

". . . dear darling Laura . . . coming away has finally given me a chance to think. I know now that I'm right. Your father and I don't belong together. Maybe we never did."

I heard Beth's shocked exclamation, and the arms that held me tightened. I tried to shut my ears, but Sophie's voice went on.

"Love's not enough when two people don't have the same temperaments, goals, values, the ways they want to live . . . got to be alone to find out what mine are—who I am. I've never been alone with me. There was always Serena, even when she wasn't there. And then your Dad, and you . . .

"Everybody needs to be able to live—be able to be a person, not just a body with 'daughter of,' 'wife of,' 'mother of,' 'employee of' stuck onto their name. Okay, maybe that's not the way you've seen me. The trouble is, it's how I have. . . . don't know yet whether I need a divorce, or a separation, but I do know I'm not coming home. I can't—"

"Stop it!" I shouted. I yanked free from Beth and catapulted toward Sophie, grabbing her so hard I knocked her sideways, tearing the letter free. I tore it

into a thousand pieces and flung them to the floor; then I couldn't breathe anymore. I was bent double, retching.

Sophie's feet ran out. Beth's arms went around me, and she rested her head against the back of mine, but she didn't say a word. Thank God.

Hours could have gone by or minutes. Then, again, there were footsteps on the stair. Sophie's, and one other's, unmistakable.

"All right," Gran's voice said quietly. "Beth, Sophie, you can leave now."

They did, without a word.

After they were gone, I swung around, my voice harsh. "I suppose Sophie told you."

Gran nodded.

"She shouldn't have. I'm okay. After all, I'm a Van Zandt, and Van Zandts are survivors, aren't we? Whether we want to be or not!" All at once, shocking even me, I began to laugh. I laughed and laughed, hiccuping, as the tears rolled down my face. "Jay's right! The way to survive is not to give a damn. Well, I don't. Not anymore!"

Gran still didn't speak. She just stood there, arms at her sides, with that suffering madonna look on her face. My voice spiraled. "What about you, Serena? Are you really so—above it all? I thought you were supposed to be crazy about Dad as a son-in-law. Or are you just crazy about maintaining the legend of Serena?

Mom was right—you really aren't made of flesh and blood!"

Serena came over and, very deliberately, slapped me across the face. I gasped, and my left hand went up to my stinging cheek, and Serena caught my right wrist in her left hand. "Stop it," she said evenly. "You're making yourself sick, and that won't change anything."

The force and the fury went out of me as if I were a pricked balloon. I sagged, and she caught me and half-led, half-carried me across the room and down the stairs. She dragged me, stumbling, over to the potter's wheel, and with her free hand scooped a lump of clay out of the bin and flung it on the wheel.

"Sit down!" Serena said, and pushed me onto the stool. She put my right foot on the pedal. "Pump!" she ordered. And I pumped, my body obeying from blind instinct.

Serena's hands centered the mound of clay. Serena's hands took mine and put them around the clay. She stood behind me, her arms around me and her fingers over mine, forcing my hands to shape the clay into an urn. "Keep pumping!" her voice whispered against my hair.

I was not in control of my own body, my own mind, or my emotions. Serena controlled my body, and it obeyed her, responding to the force that came from her like a wave. I hated her at that moment. I hated her, and I hated Mother, but mostly her because she was there and I could not resist her. But gradually my convulsive sobbing ceased, and my tension oozed away, out of my fingertips into the spinning clay. I felt my mind drifting free, as if I were half asleep. I felt my body growing quiet.

I felt Serena's arms withdraw and sensed her leaving, but my foot went on dumbly pumping at the pedal until at last it slowed, and the turntable slowed and stopped.

I sat there, spent, staring at the potter's wheel and at the little urn, grotesquely askew.

IX

Journal—Tuesday, July 5th

Vredezucht. *Place of peace. That's a hoot, as Sophie would say.*

Some peace. Some Garden of Eden. That's what I was looking for when I came here, wasn't it? Beth was right. Gran tries to play God and build a second Garden of Eden; we humans bring our private serpents into it.

Damn my mother. She's the one being the snake in the grass, not me. She's thousands of miles away and yet I'm still not free of her. She's in my blood and bone, Gran's in my blood and bone, and I'll be hearing their voices in my head till the day I die.

I'm a Van Zandt, and something ties us together no matter what. Those Van Zandts who came over in the 1620s and the ones who founded Vredezucht. *And us.*

We survive. Our hearts might be broken, but not our spirits. That's what I've been learning ever since I got here, isn't it? We pick up and we go on. Serena did. Whatever happened between her and Grandfather—I'll probably never know what but I know something did—she survived. She made her own world—to hell with anybody who didn't like it—and I can, too.

I will survive. And I'm never, ever, going to let anyone hurt me like this again.

I don't know how long I sat there. Finally I got up and scraped the clay off the turntable and dropped it back into the bin. My sides ached; I felt as if I were coming down with the flu.

I looked at the clock. It was two-thirty in the afternoon. Mechanically, I went to the kitchen and made myself a peanut butter and jelly sandwich. It gagged me, going down, but I ate it. I made a cup of tea, not as strong as the one Sophie'd made earlier, and drank it.

I went upstairs and gathered all the bits of paper I'd showered like confetti, and then I taped Mother's letter together again. It still didn't make any sense. What made sense was what Jay had told me: Don't let myself care.

Was that what Mother was doing?

How about Dad?

Dad. I wanted him to walk in the door and put the broken pieces of my life together, the way I'd put together Mother's letter, the way he used to glue together my broken toys. There was no way Dad was going to be able to glue our broken lives together, was there? A hundred pictures flashed before my eyes. Dad and Mom and I . . . laughing together, doing things together, fighting—Dad being pulled one way, Mom the other. That scene the day Gran's invitation came . . . the way Mom had balked, and Dad had talked sweet reason . . . and how Mom had burst into laughter, and given in, and thrown herself into his arms.

I'd been wrong. The chemistry wasn't gone. It was everything else that was. Chemistry alone wasn't enough. That's what Mother was trying to tell me in that letter, wasn't it?

I'd learned that already, hadn't I just, with the two Living Picture shows.

I wanted to phone Dad, but that wouldn't be right. Not if he hadn't heard from Mother yet. Surely he'd call me as soon as he did—no, first he'd call Mother, and maybe, just maybe, he'd make her change her mind. Because there was still a bond between them, I knew there was. Between *us,* I corrected myself. Kenneth J. Blair and Katherine Van Zandt Blair and Laura Serena Blair were a family. Till death did us part, and all that garbage.

I couldn't bear to sit around here till the telephone rang. Besides, I owed Beth and Sophie a thank-you for rallying around—yes, even for getting Gran. The day was so hot I was pretty sure I knew where to find them—in the river.

Fortunately at that point, it dawned on me that I was still running around in a bra and jeans. So I went upstairs again and put on my bathing suit, with a T-shirt and shorts on top. I ran downstairs and out on the porch as the mailman was coming up the steps.

"You're Miss Blair, right? Nothing today except junk mail," he said, handing it to me.

"Not worth your trip in this heat, is it?" I agreed, smiling. Then I stopped. "Wait a minute. You've already been here once today. You must have been," I said childishly, as he shook his head. "There was a letter for me in the mailbox this morning."

"I never get around this side of town till midafternoon," the mailman contradicted. Then he grinned. "Must have been that letter come for you last Saturday. I didn't know which house you were staying at then, so I gave it to Mr. Lindstrom with the rest of the Van Zandt visitors' mail. Funny he didn't get it to you earlier."

He shrugged, and saluted, and took his leave.

Very funny, because I'd seen Carl several times on Saturday. He'd even tracked me down to tell me Dad was on the phone.

Dad on the phone, sounding funny. Saying he wasn't coming for the Fourth of July after all, asking if I'd heard from Mother, telling me to remember I could always call him.

Dad had known then that this letter was coming,

and he hadn't told me. Dad must have told Carl—

I started to run, and the place where I ran to was Carl's workshop. He was there, sanding a delicate chair leg, and he looked up with a smile that faded.

"You knew, didn't you?" I demanded.

"Knew what? Laura, don't you want to sit down—"

"No, thank you," I snapped icily. "Don't give me that. Dad told you he and Mom were splitting up, didn't he? He told you to intercept any mail that might get the child upset!"

"Now wait a minute." Carl rose. "First of all, I didn't know a split was what this was all about, and I'm sorry. Second, yes, your father did say you'd be receiving a letter that would upset you. He asked me, if it arrived that day, to hold it back until today. He didn't want the holiday weekend spoiled."

"For whom? Me or Serena? Don't answer that." I slammed out and ran back to the Potter's House. It was 101 degrees in the sun, but I ran anyway. I went inside and locked the downstairs windows and the doors, so no more solicitous relations could barge in, and then I started trying to contact my father.

It took me more than an hour to do so, and all the time my own temperature was mounting, not from outside heat. Dad's calmness, when I finally tracked him down, didn't help.

"Yes, I asked a man in the office to hold the letter. He said he was a friend of yours, and he told me how happy you were, working on some show for Serena's celebration. That made me very happy. I didn't want anything to ruin that for you."

"You should have told me! You knew what Mom was doing to us, and you didn't have the decency to tell me. Why? Did you think I'd fly off the handle, or—or freak out like she does?"

Even as I said it, I had a sudden vivid picture of myself that morning. I broke out in a cold sweat, which I thanked God Dad wasn't there to see.

"No," Dad said quietly. "I thought I owed it to your mother to let her tell you herself, in her own way. If I've hurt you by doing that, I'm sorry. Laura? Punkin, I think I can finish up what I'm doing here tomorrow." He hasn't called me 'Punkin' in years, my mind registered vaguely. "I can be in Pittsburgh sometime tomorrow night, and we can fly home Thursday morning. How would that suit you?"

I hung up on him. And then, methodically, as the house rang with stillness for a minute, and then the phone began pealing, I rounded up my sunglasses and suntan oil and walked out. I went to the river, approaching the swimming spot in a roundabout way in case Beth and Sophie were there. They weren't. I stripped off my shoes and shorts and T-shirt, climbed out on the low overhanging branch, and dove.

The water hit me like Gran's slap, both comforting and shocking. I swam and swam, laps of breast strokes and side strokes and underwater, whatever I could think of that would tire me out the most.

When I came up for air after the tenth underwater lap, Jay was there beside me.

"What the hell do you think you're here for, to dole out tea and sympathy? Or do you have something more physical in mind?"

Jay raised an eyebrow. "Such language, and I thought you were so innocent. Would it help if I said I haven't the foggiest idea what you're talking about? All right," he said as I gave him a contemptuous look, "Sophie warned me you were in a black-doggish mood. Foul," he translated, seeing my puzzlement. "I assumed you were still angry because I left without telling you this weekend." He flashed that charming smile. "What difference would it have made if I had told you? I'd still have gone, but we'd both have said things we wished we hadn't. You wanted to run yourself ragged all weekend to please Serena, which I had every confidence you could do without me. I wanted to try out my pal's new Porsche on the open road, and I wanted to see the tall ships."

"And did you?" I asked nastily.

"Yes, to both things. And from what little I could gather from Sophie, you had a perfectly smashing success here. So what's wrong? You don't object to sharing the river with me, do you?" His voice took on a teasing, intimate tone.

"Don't."

"Something is wrong, isn't it?" Jay looked at me and his eyes grew serious. "I really don't know what this is about, word of honor. But it's obviously big. Want to tell me? I'm cheaper than a shrink, and I really can be every bit as discreet."

So I told him. I didn't mean to, but I told him. And in talking, I found myself growing calmer, found my thoughts taking shape and form. I didn't tell all those thoughts, though. I thanked Jay sincerely, and said I had to be going, and when he leaned forward to kiss me, I turned my face slightly so his lips landed against my cheek.

"Want me to come with you?" Jay asked.

"No. I've got some things I have to do. I'll see you later, probably." I clambered up the bank and started toward the village green, carrying my clothes. It was nearly dinnertime now, but the sun was still so hot that by the time I reached the green my suit and skin were dry. I stopped out of sight of Gran's house to put on my shorts and T-shirt and then, carrying my shoes, I went up to Gran's door and rang the bell.

Liu answered. "Yes, Mrs. Van Zandt is here. She's upstairs dressing for dinner. If you will step into the drawing room, please, I will fetch her."

"No, thank you, Liu," I said, and before I could lose my nerve I started up the stairs. Gran was in her bedroom, in a thin gray silk kimono, brushing out her hair before the pier glass. I could see my face reflected from behind her shoulder. Two faces so much alike in coloring and bone structure—

Gran's hand holding the silver brush paused in midair, but she didn't turn. "Are you all right, child?"

"Yes. Now. I'm sorry for how I acted."

"Shock affects all of us in mysterious ways. You have nothing to apologize for."

"I'm not sure I should have been all that shocked. Not when I think back, that is. I think deep down I've known the"—I swallowed hard—"the separation was coming. I've been denying it to myself."

"Yes," Gran agreed dryly, "that's what I thought."

I blushed. "I'm sorry I took it out on you. And Beth and Sophie. Gran, I've been thinking." All at once the words came in a rush. "I don't want to go back to our house, not with Mom not there. I don't even want to be with Dad. Not yet. Gran, please, would you let me stay on here? At the Potter's House?"

Silence hung in the air until the blood hammered again in my ears and I felt myself growing hot. Then Gran turned around, an inscrutable expression on her face. She looked at me and through me, and I felt as if I were being weighed and found somehow wanting.

"Just for the summer, I mean," I added lamely. "I'm sure I—I could find something here to do."

Again that silence. Then Gran's chin came up, and she gave a little nod, as if something had clicked in her own mind. "All right," she said at last, "on two conditions."

"Name them."

"That you work. I don't mean puttering around like an amateur, the way your mother has always done. I mean a regular job, whatever Carl and I can find for you to do. There's much to be done, so we're bound to find something that will suit. And that you stop feeling sorry for yourself."

My head jerked up.

"Oh, yes, you are," Gran said, exactly as if I'd spoken my denial. "You're feeling that life's been unfair to you. Well, God never promised you a rose garden. This is earth, not Eden. You're feeling overburdened—with your parents, and their expectations, and *my* expectations—with that Van Zandt heritage of having nerves on the outside of your skin that strikes one of us every generation or so. You don't think you can bear it, do you? Let me tell you something, Laura, life puts the burdens on the shoulders strong enough to bear them."

"The Gospel According to Serena Van Zandt?" I heard my own voice saying.

"No, according to Margaret Mitchell in *Gone With the Wind*. And whether you're ready to believe it now or not, one can be a survivor without growing as selfish as Scarlett O'Hara." Gran gave me a level look. "Those are my terms. Do you still want to stay?"

The words sounded cold, but there was a look in her eyes that contradicted them, that I didn't understand.

"Yes," I said, "I'll stay."

"Good." Gran turned back to the mirror again. "Now I suggest you return to the Potter's House and take a bath. I'll expect you here for dinner in an hour."

The telephone was ringing as I entered the Potter's House. I picked it up and heard Dad saying, "Operator! Operator, don't disconnect. Please keep ringing."

"It's me," I said. "I was just going to call you. I— I'm not coming home. I'm going to spend the summer here with Gran."

There was a timeless silence. Then Dad's voice, sounding almost relieved, said, "That might be best. It looks as if I'll have to be in Philadelphia most of the time through August. I can come see you. Or you can come to me. Punkin? Are you sure you're going to be all right?"

"I'm sure, Dad. You take care of yourself, too, you hear? I'm sorry for how I acted earlier." I put the phone down quietly.

When I got back to Gran's house, all the rest of the relatives were there, and they all knew about Mom and Dad. Nobody said anything about it, but I could tell. Aunt Lisa gave me a hug, and Beth kept watching me gravely. Jay and Aunt Rena provided a steady stream of light conversation. I was proud of myself for keeping up with it.

Liu cleared the table after dessert, and chairs began to be pushed back for the exodus to the drawing room.

"One moment."

Gran spoke quietly, but there was something in her voice that made everybody jump. Or in this case, freeze. Gran looked around the table, from one face to the other, with that look of vague radiance in her turquoise eyes. By now I knew the vagueness was unintentionally and totally deceptive—it came when wheels within wheels were going around inside her, when she knew exactly what she was doing. "I've been doing a lot of thinking during the past week and a half," Gran said in her silvery voice, "and I've made some plans. I want to share them with you now, for I know once we go inside you'll be buzzing over them a mile a minute."

She extended her hand to me across the table, and I took it. "Laura," Gran said, "is going to stay on in Vredezucht with me for the summer."

There was a murmur from the others, quickly checked by Gran. "This week has shown me something I suspected," she went on. "My grandchildren have been growing into young women while my back was turned, metaphorically speaking. We hardly know one another at all. So I have decided to keep them all here with me until Labor Day. It's time we found out what each of us is made of."

A gasp this time. Beth's face was white. Sophie's was interested, almost relieved. There was no "almost" about Aunt Rena's relief. Aunt Lisa looked thoughtful.

"It might be a good idea at that," she agreed. "I can paint as well here as anywhere. Wisteria Cottage is very comfortable."

"No," Gran said calmly, "my grandchildren are staying. Not the rest of you. Frankly, I've had about enough of my daughters and their personal self-expression for a time."

Aunt Rena chose to treat that as a joke. Aunt Lisa just smiled and nodded. I thought of Mother. Jay gave his charming laugh. "What about nephews, Aunt Serena? May I stay?"

"Oh, I've no doubt you'll turn up now and then," Gran said enigmatically. "Pennies always do, don't they?" She looked at Aunt Lisa again. "Go to Paris and paint, and stop worrying," Gran said. "If you've got to mother somebody, go to London and talk some sense into your sister. Lord knows she could use it. Beth will be fine here. And now for goodness sake, let's go inside and have our coffee!"

X

Gran didn't waste any time. Right after lunch on Wednesday Aunt Rena, Aunt Lisa, and Uncle Roger all left. Aunt Lisa and Uncle Roger flew to New York, from which they'd leave for London—he to his work there and she to have a sisterly talk with my mother. I'm not sure where Aunt Rena was heading, except that it was bound to be somewhere "gay and charming and amusing" (her words).

Sophie could have cared less that her mother was leaving. Beth, on the other hand, didn't seem to know whether she was relieved or sorry.

Gran informed Sophie that she was to live in what used to be the carriage house. I had a pretty good idea why. The upstairs apartment, once used for a coachman and now intended for a chauffeur, had no valuable antiques that Sophie's cigarettes could burn. It was behind the Van Zandt house, which meant that Gran could keep an eagle eye on goings-on.

"I should care!" Sophie said frankly to Beth and me. "My digs have their own outside flight of stairs, on the side away from Her Majesty's, and there are three cars downstairs in addition to that crazy surrey!"

Beth's eyes widened. Gran'll never let you take the cars!"

"I'll manage," Sophie answered airily.

Jay and I helped Sophie move from the house in which she and Aunt Rena had been staying. Considering that she'd only expected to be here for ten days, Sophie had an awful lot of clothes. I said so, and Sophie winked. "Who says I was only planning on ten days? Okay, so I didn't know for sure I'd hang around here. I darn well wasn't going to tag along after Mummy. Anyway, I've got all the stuff from boarding school, remember?"

"Considering you supposedly ran away from that school on a moment's impulse, you sure brought the kitchen sink along with you," I retorted.

Sophie shrugged. "I wasn't taking any chances on Mummy trying to send me back. Not that I think Mademoiselle would have had me." She held up a heavy navy blue gabardine school uniform, midcalf-length and high-necked. "Can you see me living like this? Give me a break!"

Beth and I helped her unpack, and afterward we went back to Wisteria Cottage, which seemed lonely with Aunt Lisa gone. Beth shivered slightly. "I'd hate this if you weren't right next door. I'm not used to being in a house alone at night. I wish you could have moved in with me."

"I'm not used to it either, but I kind of like it. The Potter's House, I mean. It's peaceful. Anyway, you heard Gran. We're supposed to keep house for ourselves. That's part of the deal."

"I can't wait," Beth said darkly, "to find out the other parts." Then she giggled. "Can you see our Sophie cooking and cleaning? Somehow I don't think Aunt Rena was a great role model for that!"

"Neither was my mother, but I manage. And Gran didn't say anything about us not cooking for each other. We could take turns; that way each of us would only have to cook one night in three."

"One night in four, probably. We're supposed to 'dine at the Van Zandt house' at least once a week. And Jay," Beth pointed out, "is probably going to find a way to hang around part of the time. You heard him."

"Yes, but I'm not depending on it. If he's hanging around us at mealtime, he can take his turn cooking," I said flatly. "Or he can take us out, if he's been eating our groceries. He seems to have plenty of ready cash."

Beth shot me a look. "You sound pretty sour."

"Nope, just realistic. I'm not about to count on him again. At least Gran overlooked period authenticity enough to have dishwashers in the houses. Not to mention washers and dryers. That makes up for not having a shower. I only brought one small suitcase of clothes here with me."

"So did I, but Mother's sending me more before she leaves for London. Can't your dad ship you some from Elm Grove when he gets there? Or you could phone him and ask for some money to go shopping. Or you could ask Gran."

"I'm not asking Gran for handouts," I said shortly. "I'm not sure I want to ask Dad, either."

Beth looked at me and saw a lot more than I wanted. "Oh," she said. "Well, I've got a shower. You can come next door and use it."

I was beginning to get the feeling that in asking Gran if I could stay here, I'd avoided one can of worms only to open Pandora's box instead.

I was sure of it at dinner. Sophie and Beth and I showed up at Gran's as ordered, and it was a lot different from our earlier dinners there. For one thing, it was just the three of us and Gran. Great-Aunt Alexandra wasn't feeling well and had gone to bed early, Gran said. For another thing, Liu wasn't there. Dinner, which was waiting for us on the screened porch, was a chicken pot pie and salad.

"Did you enjoy it?" Gran inquired when we were finished.

"It was super. A lot more my style than all the finicky sauces and fingerbowls," Sophie said forthrightly.

"Good. I cooked it myself from my mother's recipe. Liu needed a vacation, so I put him on a plane this afternoon." Gran looked at us. "I'm doing my own cooking the rest of the summer. Except that on Friday nights, when you three girls dine here, each of the four of us will cook the meal in turn. I know Beth is going to be a ballerina and Sophie a rock singer, but knowing how to cook won't hurt you. From what I hear from friends in the performing arts, it could be a lifesaver for you when you're on the road. I haven't heard yet what career Laura intends, but I'm sure she's already discovered that it's unfortunate for a career woman to grow up not knowing how to produce pleasant meals."

Ouch, I thought, remembering Mother's grudging efforts whenever Gran had blown into town. Mother had never learned how to cook decently; it was a safe bet that Aunt Rena hadn't either. It occurred to me that Gran intended to use this summer making up with her granddaughters for deficiencies in the raising of her daughters.

"Now, as to your work this summer." Gran produced a list. "Sit down, Sophie. You didn't expect to get away with doing nothing, did you? Just remember I'm saving you from Swiss summer school."

She proceeded to outline her arrangements. I was to work under Carl in the furniture refinishing workshop. Sophie was to learn to run the switchboard in the office. "I expect you to look presentable for a business office, and I expect politeness and decent English. British English will be quite satisfactory, but no slang. And no language that would shock the natives."

For Beth, Gran had lined up a dance instructor once connected with the Kirov Ballet. "I'm well aware that dancers must devote all their time to practice, that the practice is their work. I expect you to treat it as such, and to present a recital at the end of the summer. You will each be paid the same salaries other resident apprentices in the Village receive. If you budget carefully, you should finish the summer with some savings. And since none of you came prepared in the matter of clothes, I will also give you a clothing allowance. The business manager will have those checks for you in the office tomorrow morning, and the van can take you to Pittsburgh Saturday for shopping. Now go home and get a good night's sleep, and report to your assignments at nine tomorrow morning."

Now I knew what Mother meant when she said Gran was a force of nature, like a tidal wave.

Mother. I wasn't going to think about Mother.

I ought to write her; I knew she'd be anxiously waiting for my reaction to her letter. But I didn't do it. I went back to the Potter's House and wrote in the notebook I'd been using as a journal when I came here.

"Journal. Darn you, Mother, you're pulling strings in me even when you and I didn't know it."

When I went to bed, very late, the lamp in Beth's

bedroom was still on. I didn't know what she was thinking. She'd been very quiet all the way home.

So in jeans and an old shirt, I reported to Carl in the workshop the next morning. I already knew I'd like the workshop, which was sunlit and peaceful, and I expected to like working for Carl. What I didn't expect was how much I liked the work itself. Repairing and refinishing antiques as valuable as these had to be done in the old ways—hand sanding and hand rubbing, no power tools. Stripping and sanding and planing had a rhythm, just as modeling on the potter's wheel did. I found myself drifting into the same floating-free state that Gran and the wheel had induced in me that awful day.

Other workers were in and out: student apprentices, craftsmen in their twenties and thirties with calloused hands, old men with a lifetime of skill in their worn fingers. By the time five o'clock came, I was very tired, but I'd decided this was a perfect place to spend the summer.

As I was walking home, I heard my name called. An unfamiliar figure was hurrying toward me across the green. "Laura! Do wait! I'm not up to running!"

I did a double take. "Sophie?" Her hair was plain brown, and she wore a plain shirt and skirt and an exasperated expression. "Where on earth did you get that outfit?"

"Revolting, isn't it? I borrowed it from Gran's secretary. Definitely not me, but with Serena in her present mood I didn't dare show up in any of my own rags. Look, Laura, you will be a lamb, won't you, and save my life?"

"How?" I asked warily.

"You don't have a date or anything, do you? Jay's gone off someplace, so you're my only hope with a car. I want you to drive me somewhere on the highway to find a shopping mall. I've got to get me something better than this to wear before tomorrow. I'll buy us dinner. My treat."

What I really wanted to do was take a swim in the river, and sleep. But Sophie was right about the shopping. "We'd better take Beth, too," I said.

Beth, when we found her, shook her head. "You two go. I don't feel like eating."

"Neither do I, but what's that got to do with it?" Sophie murmured to me when we finally gave up pleading. "The kid looks like she's on a hunger strike or something. You don't think there's anything really wrong with her, do you?"

"I don't know." I was more worried than I wanted to admit.

Sophie and I found a mall, and I bought pants and tops and a couple of dresses, and Sophie bought herself what she called a "Marks and Spencer wardrobe," by which she meant plain everyday working girl, inexpensive. Quite a change for Sophie, I thought, grinning to myself. Sophie was acting for all the world like an actress buying costumes for a role.

"Thanks a whole heap," I retorted when Sophie asked me for the third time what I'd choose in the way of tops or skirts or shoes.

"Don't be so black-doggish," Sophie said. "You know you don't dress high style. Well, not Eurostyle, anyway," she amended.

"We live in different worlds, I know."

"You *are* angry. Sorry, no offense intended. I really want your help, actually."

"In preference to Gran's?" I inquired. Sophie snickered.

"Well, at least we're in the same generation. I must say, Serena's going in for a good bit of 'do as I say, not as I do.' When has she ever dressed like ordinary people?"

"When has she ever been ordinary people? She's Serena Van Zandt."

"All right, all right," Sophie said soothingly. "Let's go tie on the feed bags, shall we?"

We found an Italian family restaurant in the mall and ordered pizza. Sophie's mood had changed; she ordered pizza with everything and flirted with the waiter and in general behaved as if her hair was still multicolor. But when the pizza came, reeking with garlic and anchovies, she didn't eat much.

"Are you sure you're okay?" I asked when she came

back from the girls' room. "You look kind of green."

"It's the war paint." Sophie had put on bright lipstick and green eyeshadow. "That pizza's too much for a hot night, is all."

"You could have ordered something else," I said, after telling the waiter to wrap the remaining half pizza for us to take home.

"If you're going to start preaching at me, I might as well have mooched dinner at Gran's." Sophie slung her purse strap over her shoulder. "Come on, let's go home. I have to be at that bloody switchboard again at nine tomorrow."

In the car her mood changed again, and we rode without speaking. Then, as the car headlights reached the village green, she turned to me. "Feel like giving me a cuppa char and some chat?" Beneath the mock Cockney accent Sophie sounded a bit forlorn.

"Sure," I said. I parked in front of the Potter's House, and we went inside. I filled the kettle and measured tea into the fat brown teapot while Sophie perched on the stool by the potter's wheel and watched.

"Ever try this thing?" she asked, glancing at the wheel.

"A couple of times. Gran made me. It's not my thing."

"Mine, neither. She tried with me, too." Sophie's voice was almost wistful. "It must be nice to have a *thing*."

"Come on! Since when have you ever wanted a career?"

"Who's talking career? I mean something you're good at, something that matters. Like Aunt Lisa's painting and Aunt Kay's writing. And Beth's dancing."

"I don't have a *thing,* as you call it."

"Oh, you do," Sophie said with sureness. "You may not know what it is yet. But you'll never be like me and Mummy, tearing around looking for experiences to fill up the void."

I'd never heard Sophie talk like this before. "I'm not sure where my mom fits into those descriptions," I said carefully. "But if you really want to find something that's yours to do—"

The teakettle shrieked loudly. Almost at the same moment, the telephone rang. "I'll get that," Sophie said, scooping up the phone.

I started to fill the teapot. "Potter's House," I heard Sophie say, for all the world like a switchboard operator. And then, in her old excited voice, "Aunt Kay!"

I swung around, gesturing violently.

"Sophie here," my cousin said. "I'm so glad—" Then she saw me signaling and frowned. "Wait a minute, Aunt Kay," she said and put her hand over the receiver. "What's the matter with you?" she hissed at me.

"I don't want to talk to her."

"Laura—"

"*No.* I mean it!"

Sophie took her hand off the mouthpiece. "Sorry, Aunt Kay," she said glibly. "The teakettle here was boiling . . . Laura?" Ostentatiously Sophie swung around so her back was to me. "Sorry, I don't see her. I just came in from shopping and I'm making meself a cuppa char . . . I wish we were together, too. You have a cuppa for me over there, right? Since Laura's not available, I'd best ring off . . . Yes, I'll tell her. Love you."

She hung up and swung back around. "May I ask," she inquired distinctly, "what that was supposed to prove?"

"It wasn't supposed to prove anything. I just wasn't ready to talk to her." I pushed a steaming mug of tea toward Sophie. "Forget it. I'm going to write her soon, really. Put your feet up and let your hair down on whatever you wanted to talk to me about."

"I've changed my mind," Sophie said grandly. "Why should I come to you for advice on my life when you can't even manage your own? No thanks, I can see myself home."

She made an exit, leaving me feeling like I can't say what.

XI

DINNER I COOKED FOR GRAN

Transylvanian Borscht

2 lb. lean beef, cut in cubes, all fat removed
4 or 5 carrots, peeled, cut in chunks
3 large white turnips, peeled, cut in chunks
3 medium potatoes, peeled, cut in chunks
3 medium onions, sliced
2 cups white cabbage, shredded
2 cups red cabbage, shredded
2 16-oz. cans cooked sliced beets
beef bouillon as needed (about 5 cups)
2 tbs. tomato paste
1/4 cup paprika
1/4 cup black caraway seeds

¹/₄ cup brown caraway seeds
3 tbs. honey
3 tbs. vinegar

Drain canned beets and set aside. Keep the juice!
*Put beef, beet juice, tomato paste, and bouillon to cover
into soup pot.* (Note: I used a total of 2 cans of the kind
you dilute.) *Bring to boil; then reduce heat and simmer,
covered, for 1 hour, skimming frequently.*

*Add everything else, including drained beets. Simmer
until everything's fork-tender* (took me an hour). *If more
liquid is needed, add more bouillon.*

Bring to boil again. Ladle into big *bowls. Serve with a
dollop of sour cream on top, and pass chopped chives and
the pepper mill.*

(Note: We had enough left over for Sophie and Beth
and me to eat the second night. It was even better left
over!)

It was a week before Jay showed up again. In that week
a lot of things happened.

Mother called twice more. Once I really wasn't around,
and she left a message for me at the office. The second
time was when Beth and I were eating dinner at the
Potter's House, and a sixth sense told me to have Beth
answer the phone. Beth, like Sophie, fudged about my
whereabouts. Unlike Sophie, she didn't lecture me. She
just gazed at me with a grave, troubled expression.

"Don't you start," I said.

"Start what?"

"That martyred madonna look. It's pure Gran."

"Thanks a whole heap," Beth said with dignity. And then, "If you want to avoid Aunt Kay's calls, you'd better write her. Overnight mail."

So I did. It was more a note, actually. I told Mother I'd received her letter, and I loved her. And that I needed to have her "give me space." All things considered, Mother was in no position to complain about that request. I took the letter to the office the next day, choosing a time when Sophie would be out to lunch, and asked the secretary to mail it for me. Carl was there at the time, and he saw the address, but if he had opinions on the subject he didn't voice them.

Bless Carl, I thought more than once. He was a good boss. I don't mean easy; more than once he made me do work over till I had it right. But he was fair, and the atmosphere in his workshop was the same atmosphere Gran created—a peace that was "dynamic, not inert."

I couldn't help picking up jargon like that, working on one of Gran's projects. Little by little the meaning of the phrase seeped into my consciousness.

I had no idea whether Sophie or Beth had the same feeling about where they were working. Beth was a regular clam. Sophie talked a blue streak, when the grownups weren't around, but under the chitchat she had a silence, too. I didn't know what her problem was, but I could take a good guess as to Beth's—as far as the dance work Gran had assigned to her was concerned, I mean.

Madame Karhanova, the teacher Gran had unearthed, was a real Tartar. She was half as old as time, and very thin, so thin that the yellowed skin seemed stretched across her skeleton. Her eyes burned like a fanatic's, and what she was fanatic about was the Russian style of dance and discipline.

"I've heard about it before," Beth murmured, rubbing her instep. "But I've never run across it. Not to this extent." We were up in Sophie's digs on Monday night, eating spaghetti with sauce out of a jar.

Sophie looked at the bruises on Beth's toes. "Why don't you complain?" she demanded practically.

"I wouldn't dare!"

Sophie had overcooked the spaghetti and burned the sauce. "I didn't feel like eating anyway," she muttered, dumping her plateful into the garbage pail. "Oh, well, if I'm a rotten enough cook, Gran won't expect me to produce for her. I think I'll turn in. Laura, why don't you drive Beth out on the highway and find her some food?"

Neither of us felt like doing that. Beth and I settled on double-dip ice cream cones from the old-fashioned soda fountain in town. We walked home licking them through the summer twilight.

"What are you going to cook for Gran?" Beth asked. She and Sophie had already decided I should be the first sacrificial lamb in that job.

"I don't know. I've got till Wednesday to decide."

"You could call your mother and ask for suggestions," Beth said innocently.

"Are you kidding? You've tasted my mother's cooking! Anyway, in her present mood she's apt to suggest rat poison."

Beth made a point of letting that pass. I looked at her, then away. "Okay, I know I'm acting like a spoiled brat. That's why I don't want to talk to her till I can handle it. I don't want to say things I'll regret. I don't want to have to answer the questions I know she'll ask. You know what that's like."

Beth didn't answer that, either. My words hung in the air, gaining reason by the fact that they were not contradicted.

I was worried about Beth's bruises, and how drawn she'd looked after her Monday class. So Tuesday afternoon I arranged with Carl to take a shorter lunch break and leave early. I "just happened" to drop by the Opera House before Beth's afternoon class was through.

I knew better than to barge in, but the closed door of the rehearsal room had a glass pane in it. And Madame Karhanova made no attempt to keep her voice down.

"No! You stupid fool, how often must I tell you?"

She thumped the floor with her stick. "Slower on the *developé,* and the head *so.* And the feet out, *out!*"

This time the stick banged across Beth's instep.

I turned away, feeling sick.

I figured Beth might need some company after her class, and I managed to be on the front porch as Beth approached, dragging. "Come have some iced tea," I called. "And I made tuna fish salad. There's plenty, if you want to eat here."

Beth accepted gratefully. "So how's class?" I asked, carefully casual, as we sat on the porch, eating with our feet propped up on the railings.

"Okay, I guess."

"Is Madame as good as Gran says she is? She looks like a tyrant."

"She's one of the old-school Russians. They have high standards. But that's what it takes to be a dancer." Beth lifted her feet down, wincing slightly. "You know what I'd like to do? Go swimming in the river before it gets too dark."

So we went and changed, and the water felt good after the clammy humidity of the day. Sophie didn't appear, but Carl did and a few of the other apprentices. We had fun, diving until the light vanished and then floating dreamily. After a while lightning crackled.

"Heat lightning," Carl said, looking up. "The barometric pressure's rising. We'll probably have a storm tomorrow."

On Wednesday morning the sky was overcast and the air was still. Heat lay like a blanket in the trees as I walked to work. Varnish wouldn't dry. In midmorning the workshop telephone rang. "Laura," Carl called. And then, hand over the mouthpiece, "No, it's not your mother." I turned scarlet and took the receiver. The caller was Gran.

"Laura, darling. I'm calling to make sure we're set for dinner. Sophie tells me you're the chef tonight. Do you plan to cook here?"

"I'm going to cook at the Potter's House, and then drive things over." Cooking for Gran was awesome enough without having to do it under her eyes.

"Of course. I keep forgetting you have a car. I'll expect you at six, then. Have you had a chance to talk to Beth and Sophie as I asked you?"

"No. Not yet."

"Then make a chance. Soon. I am becoming quite worried about Elizabeth." Gran put down her receiver and I did likewise, my face stinging. I was beginning to resent imperial commands, in spite of the graciousness with which they were expressed.

I also felt awkward, with the other apprentices and employees, even Carl, being both an apprentice and Serena's granddaughter. Employee use of the phone was frowned on during working hours, and yet Gran called me on personal business. I'll be fair; the awkwardness was all on my side. Nobody else did anything to make me feel that way. Carl even came over, as I was getting ready to leave for lunch, and carefully took me aside before he spoke. "I couldn't help hearing. If you're cooking for Serena you deserve the afternoon off. No arguments," he said, smiling. "I know you'll make the work up some other time."

I left gratefully. By now the sky was an odd yellow-gray, and before I finished doing my grocery shopping thunder rolled and then the heavens opened. The rain pelted me as I ran across the green, the brown paper bags disintegrating in my arms.

The sky had turned to leaden twilight, and the wet hair streaming in my face blinded my eyes. I didn't see the lights glowing in the windows of the Potter's House until I was stumbling up the steps. Dad, was my first thought. And then the front door opened, and an unmistakable figure stood silhouetted in the doorway.

Jay.

Jay, coming forward to take the sodden bundles from my arms. Jay, laughing, saying, "If I'd known how to hot-wire your auto, I'd have come to get you. I phoned the workshop, and Lindstrom told me where you'd gone." Jay, sending me upstairs like a child to shower and change while he unpacked the groceries.

When I came down again, wrapped in a terry cloth robe and toweling my hair dry, Jay had built a fire in the fireplace. "Nice on a raw day, and the temperature's dropping. You haven't had lunch, have you? I'm famished." He was making omelets at the kitchen stove.

"What brought you back out of the blue?" I asked.

"Filial duty. Grandfilial, actually. I'm taking Grand-mère out to dinner." That was his name for Great-Aunt Alexandra. Jay paused, spatula in hand. "Have you seen her lately? Is it just me, or is she failing?"

"I think she is."

Jay was silent for a moment. "Just have to show the old dear a good time tonight, won't I? Put the teakettle on, there's a good girl. You wouldn't like to come along for the family dinner, would you?"

I indicated the groceries. "I'm putting on a family dinner of my own, for Gran."

"Then I won't try to tempt you away. Not this time." Jay's tone was intimate and teasing.

"Jay, don't."

"All right then," Jay said and stayed on through the afternoon to help me cook.

He asked me what I was producing for the grand dinner, and I said it wasn't grand, just a casserole, half something I remembered Dad making and half inspiration. It didn't have a name, but Jay, seeing the beets and cabbage and the two kinds of caraway seeds I'd found in the local herb shop, laughed and named it Transylvanian Borscht. "Only ve need ze—how you say it? Ze Count Dracula to make the night complete."

He nibbled my neck, and I told him to behave himself. Actually, at that point I was feeling a little breathless, and not from the heat. Not from the weather, that is.

By the time my soup-casserole-stew had simmered itself to fragrant tenderness, the rain had let up some. I dressed up, properly, in one of my new dresses. Jay rode over to Gran's with me. Or rather, he drove my mother's old heap while I balanced the stewpot on a pile of towels and newspapers in my lap. Jay stopped at the grocery store and returned in triumph. "Black bread and sour cream. You can't be *mitteleuropean* without them!"

We invaded Gran's kitchen with our booty, and while I put the casserole in the oven, Jay disappeared, to return resplendent in gray slacks, striped tie, and a blue blazer bearing the crest of his old school. Gran came downstairs, in an Indian cotton caftan, guiding Great-Aunt Alexandra, who looked splendid and very frail.

"Do be careful, Jay," she said warningly.

Jay smiled. "Of which, Aunt Serena? Grandmère or your Mercedes?"

"Both." Gran was not amused.

Jay helped Great-Aunt Alexandra out to the car gallantly, with us and Sophie and Beth as audience. "I'll take good care of her," he promised Gran. "Be seeing you."

He smiled again, that charming carefree smile. The smile and those last words were directed at me, not Gran, and I didn't like the way my heart and backbone melted.

XII

Everybody liked my Transylvanian Borscht, but only Gran and I ate much of it. Beth just picked at her food as usual, and to my surprise so did Sophie. On all previous visits that I could remember, Sophie had eaten like a football player.

The evening broke up early, for we all were tired. "Good healthy weariness from work," Gran said bracingly. Sophie groaned, and I saw Beth wince. Gran laughed. "You're young! Working hard this summer won't kill you." She tried to draw us out about our daily jobs, and Sophie told indiscreet but very funny stories about Gran's office employees, and I talked about furniture refinishing and tried to avoid talking about people. Beth avoided talking, period.

"I think you ought to tell Gran about Madame. And don't pretend you don't know what I mean," I told Beth firmly as I drove her home.

"Cut it out! I just can't take any more." To my dismay, Beth's voice cracked.

"I wish you'd let me help," I said gently.

"The best way you can help is by letting me alone. Remember what you said about needing space to think in? Well, so do I." Beth subsided in silence till we reached Wisteria Cottage and went inside without another word.

The next morning, very early, the telephone rang. I picked it up apprehensively.

"Laura! Come away with me and be my love!" Jay's voice said exuberantly. "To the ends of the earth, or at least to Pittsburgh."

I couldn't help laughing. "I have to work, you idiot!"

"Where?"

"The antiques workshop. I'm a wage slave, didn't you hear?"

Jay chuckled. "Oh, *there*. Then you can easily—"

"No, I can't. I won't. I'll see you after work, if you want."

"We'll see," Jay said enigmatically.

To my dismay, he showed up at the workshop in midmorning, every inch the young gentleman at leisure in a silk shirt, sports jacket, and white ducks. I was in stained jeans and a bleached-out T-shirt, struggling with old varnish crusted on the carved legs of a chair. Two of the other apprentices looked at him and me, and exchanged amused glances.

Jay spoke with Carl. Then Carl looked at me and

beckoned, a quizzical expression on his face. "Mrs. Van Zandt wants you to do some errands in Pittsburgh for her. Tremaine will drive you."

I followed Jay outside, at a loss for words.

"Wasn't I clever?" Jay asked with satisfaction when we were underway in Gran's Mercedes. "I could see Grandmère needed some dresses more suited to the Pennsylvania summer, and since this weather's too hot for her to go out in, I persuaded Aunt Serena you should be her personal shopper."

"Jay! I can't pick out clothes for Great-Aunt Alexandra!"

"Don't worry, I can," Jay said calmly. And he was right. After a hair-raisingly fast ride to Pittsburgh, Jay steered me into exactly the right, awfully expensive shops. He had a list of sizes, and he chose the dresses, delicate sheers in soft pastel colors with hand detailing and prices that almost made me faint. He paid for our purchases from a thick roll of bills.

"Now," he said masterfully, after the boxes were locked in the trunk of the Mercedes, "I'm taking you to lunch. Then you're going to help me shop."

"For what?"

"You'll see."

For what turned out to be a Mercedes convertible. Bright red, with gunmetal leather upholstery, straight off the floor of the showroom while everybody bowed and scraped. "I decided against a Porsche after all," Jay said carelessly, peeling off enough five hundred dollar bills to choke a cow.

"Jay, how on earth—"

He jabbed me in the ribs. "Gift from Grandmère," he said later, when we were having sundaes at Houlihan's while we waited for the car to be prepped and the licensing and insurance to be taken care of. "I was talking at dinner last night about how inconvenient it was not having a car to drive in this country. Especially since I'm going to be staying in the States all summer."

I felt a pressure gathering around my heart. "I didn't know you were going to stay all summer."

"Neither did I, before I got here." Jay's eyes twinkled, then grew grave. "To tell you the truth, with Uncle Roger back in England, I don't feel it would be too wise to go off and leave her, but of course I didn't tell her that. I said I had friends at Saratoga and on Long Island who were after me to visit. But I'll pop in and out of Vredezucht after decent intervals elsewhere." Those eyes twinkled at me again. "You don't mind, do you?"

"Tell me about the car," I said severely.

"When Grandmère heard all that, she insisted on giving me money for a car." Jay started to laugh. "Do you know, she actually had that wad tucked inside her corset? I thought ladies only did that in old novels!"

"There aren't many ladies like Great-Aunt Alexandra."

"She's one of a kind," Jay agreed. "So is Serena."

It wasn't till we were sauntering back to the showroom that it occurred to me to ask how we were getting the new car back with us. "You'll drive it," Jay said as a matter of course. "You have your driver's license with you, don't you?"

"Yes, but—"

"No buts. You'd rather be responsible for my car than Serena's, wouldn't you? Don't worry! I can almost guarantee you I'll put the first dents in it myself!"

I never was so petrified driving in my life. Particularly since I stayed well within the speed limit, and Jay did not, which meant he was back in Vredezucht long before me. He was waiting in front of the Potter's House when I pulled up. "How about a swim and then dinner?" he asked.

"No way! I'm going back to the workshop to apologize for being kidnapped! And no, I can't have dinner with you."

"Why not?"

"I just can't." I was not about to say I thought I'd spent more hours with him today than were a good idea.

Jay grinned, kissed me lightly, and roared off in a way guaranteed to bring the new Mercedes its first dent in the near future. I got in Mom's old car and drove to the workshop.

It was later than I'd thought. Everyone had left but

Carl, who was cleaning brushes and whistling to himself. "How was life among the effete rich?" he asked, his eyes twinkling.

"You wouldn't believe it if I told you. Carl, about today, I'm sorry."

"Forget it. If you'd been a spoiled kid trying to cop out, I'd have come down hard. But I could tell it wasn't your idea."

"Having me work here wasn't your idea either, and I know it."

Carl stopped whistling and came over. "Laura, look at me. Look at me. You're thinking about the bad press your grandmother has, aren't you? Serena Van Zandt, Patroness of the Arts, et cetera? Do you really think that little, not just of her but of yourself and me?"

"What do you mean?" I asked, startled.

"I knew about your grandmother's rep before I interviewed for this job: autocratic, follows her own rules, all the rest. I'm not saying I wouldn't have taken the job even if that had been true; working here was too valuable an experience to miss, in a lot of ways. But I sure wouldn't have enjoyed working here as much. And I wouldn't have taken you on as an apprentice if I hadn't already been convinced you could hack it according to the rules. I saw your leadership and dedication with that picture show, remember?"

"But it was Gran's idea." What was that word Mother slung around, the one that meant giving people undeserved preference because they were family? "It's—nepotism."

Carl looked at me with a whimsical expression that made me feel as if I were all of ten years old. "Laura, haven't you been here long enough by now to realize your grandmother doesn't give people things they don't deserve? She gambles on the potential she sees in people, and she's a darn good judge of character. I found that out fast. She'd never have put you in here if she hadn't known it was a good idea."

"Good for the workshop? Or just good for me?"

"Both. Now get out of here. I'll see you at nine tomorrow."

As I drove home, I passed Beth, who was walking slowly along. Limping, rather. I pulled over. "Get in. What happened to you?"

Beth slid in gratefully. "I twisted my ankle when I came down from a *grand jeté*. It's nothing."

"The heck it is. Your ankles have been weak an awful lot lately, haven't they? You'd better stay off that leg for a day or so."

"Don't be ridiculous," Beth said with dignity. "Dancers are like athletes. They don't give in when they hit the wall of pain."

"Who says so? Madame?"

"Everybody knows it." Beth giggled tiredly. "Not that that stopped her from reminding me anyway."

"I think you ought to talk to Gran about it."

"No!" Beth swiveled to face me, her eyes alarmed. "And don't you either, understand? If I can't take Madame's old-school methods—"

"You mean tyranny."

"Okay, tyranny. That's what it takes to make ballet so beautiful. The discipline. Endurance. If I can't take it, I'll never be a dancer. I've got to find out. So swear you won't say a word about any of this to Gran—or anyone."

"But Beth—"

"Swear!"

Beth looked so panic-stricken that I promised reluctantly. "I just wish you'd let me do *something* to help," I added.

"Okay, if you're determined to be a mother hen, you can ask me over for leftovers," Beth said, more lightly.

"You got it."

I made Beth soak her ankle while I phoned Sophie. Sophie said leftover Transylvanian Borscht was better than having to cook herself, and she'd be right over. My concoction tasted even better the second day, and I actually got the other two to eat. Sophie had already seen Jay's Mercedes, and she pumped me for details of the shopping tour. We had a hilarious time at the expense of poor Jay and Great-Aunt Alexandra.

Beth wiped her eyes. "I've never laughed as much as I have with you two."

"Even us barmy souls have our uses," Sophie said.

"Come on, cripple, I'm putting you to bed." She marched Beth out, but gently, for the ankle had begun to swell.

I was tired, but in no way sleepy. I puttered around, putting the house to bed and thinking about what Carl had said. I was just putting the downstairs lights out when the screen door opened and Jay came in.

"You don't want to go up yet. Pour us some iced tea and let's sit a while on the porch." He went to the refrigerator and calmly helped himself.

"What would you have done if I hadn't had any tea in there?" I asked, getting down glasses.

"Ah, but I knew you would. You're dependable. That's one of the things I find irresistible about you." There was a mischievous gleam in Jay's eyes as he put a faint emphasis on that word, *one*. I ignored the bait and went to sit on the porch swing. Jay followed and sat beside me.

"Grandmère was really pleased with the shopping you did for her."

"That you did, you mean. You didn't need me."

"Oh, yes, I did." Jay's tone was half teasing, half caressing. He reached out a finger and brushed a strand of hair off my neck. "Laura Serena Blair, what I would have missed if I hadn't accepted Aunt Serena's invitation."

"Yes, you'd have missed out on a new Mercedes," I said dryly.

"And she has a tongue as sharp as her grandmother's,

too," Jay murmured. "That's not what I meant, and you know it. Seriously, I think it's a good thing for everybody that we all came. Grandmère's certainly better off here with her sister. One of those VIPs from New York gave Cousin Lisa a juicy commission. Sophie's calming down—or at least she's not chasing rock stars. Beth's getting ballet lessons *à la Russe*. You're getting a breather from a bad scene at home."

"And learning furniture refinishing. I really like it."

"Of course," Jay said enigmatically. "Serena always knows what people need, doesn't she?" He chuckled. "Too bad she didn't come up with a suitable new man for Cousin Rena."

"Jay, you're awful."

"Of course," Jay said complacently, "that's my charm."

"Is that what Gran invited you for?" I murmured wickedly.

"Come on! We all know what Serena rounded us up for. Too bad for me that I don't fit the specifications."

"Cheap labor for the village?" I looked him over with mock severity. "I'm afraid you're not dependable enough."

"Too right I'm not, but not just for entry-level jobs. Serena's looking for an heir apparent, somebody she can pass the responsibility for the family and the village on to. If you ask me, Serena's given up hope that any of her daughters, except maybe Lisa, would measure up, so she's checking out the younger generation."

Unaccountably my heart started to pound. "That's not funny," I said shortly.

"It's not, and I didn't mean it to be." Jay stretched, and rose, and stood looking down at me with an odd expression. "You really are an innocent, aren't you, Laura? That's probably one more thing in your favor. Right now it's odds on you're in front of the race."

"Jay," I said carefully, "I think you'd better go."

Jay bent and kissed me, a kiss that was like the one in the Living Picture. When he released me, both of us were breathing hard.

"Think about it," he said. "And for what it's worth, my money's on you. You and Serena are cut from the same bolt of cloth, whether you recognize that yet or not."

XIII

Jay went, leaving me sitting there in the dark feeling uncomfortable about a lot of things. As soon as the taillights of the Mercedes vanished around the green, Sophie came across the lawn from Wisteria Cottage.

"Any more of that iced tea?" she asked.

"In the refrigerator," I answered, my voice muffled. I went to get it, and Sophie followed me in. "What was Jay here for? Beside the obvious," she asked without preamble.

"I don't know what you're talking about," I said with as much dignity as I could muster. "He came to give me Great-Aunt Alexandra's thanks for helping with the shopping."

Sophie snorted. "Great-Aunt Alexandra probably doesn't even realize the shopping took place. She's in Spaceville half the time, haven't you noticed? I wonder how aware she was when she authorized that Mercedes."

"Sophie, that's not fair!"

"Isn't it?" Sophie raised an eyebrow. "You wait and see. I hope that tender scene on the porch just now's enough to last you for a while, because we probably won't be seeing so much of our dear cousin now that he's gotten what he wanted. Don't look at me like that. I mean the car."

"Jay isn't like that." I meant the words to come out strong and firm, but my voice betrayed me. Sophie looked at me and gave me a knowing smile.

"I hope for your sake you haven't really fallen for him. Jay's a doll. He's also a heel. I should know. I've had lots of experience with the type." She perched on the stool at the potter's wheel and lit a cigarette, throwing the burnt match carelessly on the floor. I stooped for it. "Laura Serena, the picker-up of pieces," she mocked. "Too bad you're too much of a baby to pick up mine."

"What's that supposed to mean?"

"Nothing. I wish Aunt Kay were here, that's all."

"You could go to London, if you and my mother are so much on the same wavelength." My voice had an edge I couldn't help.

"London," Sophie said, "is the last place I want to be right now. Even less than this place." She inhaled deeply. "I can't help it if you and your mum aren't on the same wavelength; she'd be a hell of a lot more good for me than anyone else around."

She blew out a cloud of smoke and stared into space, and I saw that her eyes were wet.

"Sophie, what is it?" I asked softly. "I wish you'd tell me. Maybe I could help."

"You! You're a baby. A baby's the last thing I need." Suddenly, shockingly, she started to laugh. She laughed and laughed, hugging herself and leaning against the potter's wheel to keep from falling.

"I'll get Gran." I reached for the telephone in alarm.

"No!" Sophie jumped down and actually grabbed the receiver from my hand. It dropped back in its cradle with a thump, and Sophie walked away, still hugging herself, bent over but with her head thrown back.

"Sophie, what is it? Tell me! Are you sick?"

"You could put it that way." Sophie started to laugh. "If you must know, I think I've gone and gotten myself knocked up."

I looked at her blankly. Sophie sat down and lit another cigarette. "Sorry, I keep forgetting you don't know Brit slang. I think I'm pregnant."

All I could say, dumbly, was "You couldn't be."

"You're not that naive. Yes, I could." Sophie's hand, holding the cigarette, shook, but her voice had steadied. "I've been afraid I was, and now I'm almost sure. Now do you see why I wish Aunt Kay were here? She's the only one in the family who might not have hysterics."

"I'm not having hysterics," I said steadily. My mouth

was dry. I went to the sink and filled the teakettle, and put it on the stove. Hot tea in a time of trouble—it was a family tradition. Then I went to the sofa and made Sophie sit down with me, after I'd first closed the doors and windows. This was one conversation we didn't need floating on the clear night air. "What are you going to do?" I asked Sophie.

"Darned if I know. I can't think straight. My thoughts keep chasing around like rats in a cage."

"Are you going to get married?"

"Don't make me laugh! Can you see me married? Even supposing the guy would want to? Knowing the kind of men I fall for, do you think either one of us would make a good parent?"

The kettle shrilled. I went and made tea, and carried it back to the coffee table. Sophie was sitting blowing smoke rings abstractedly, but she wasn't shaking now. "Ta." Her hands closed around the hot teacup gratefully.

"Sophie?" I said tentatively when I couldn't bear the silence anymore. "If you are pregnant, who's the father?"

There was another, very heavy silence, and I was sure I'd gone too far. Then Sophie turned her head toward me, slowly. She looked me up and down, her expression odd. "You great baby, who do you think? Who was I hanging around with in London? Not to mention here, until the roving eye fixed itself on you instead? Wake up!"

Jay. It couldn't be Jay.

I didn't know I'd breathed the words aloud until Sophie gave a small, very old laugh. "Wise up, Laura! Nobody can be that naive in this day and age. Jay's only a second or third cousin, and we're both normal and healthy, for heaven's sake. What do you think was going on in London? What do you think Aunt Kay's probably up to there right now?"

I slapped her, hard, across the face.

For a minute we just stared at each other. Then Sophie set the teacup down. Her hand was unsteady; the cup clattered against the saucer. Her voice was unsteady, too. "I shouldn't have said that about your mum. I'm sorry. But Laura, you'd better face up to it. Aunt Kay was unhappy here, and you know it. And she's still good-looking, and alive, and young."

And she's felt Dad neglected her, the computer that was my mind added. She feels like she's getting old and hasn't lived.

"I don't believe it," my voice said doggedly. "And I don't believe Jay's the father of your baby."

"Believe what you want." Sophie wiped her eyes and looked at me directly. "Look, while we're letting it all out, what's really bugging you? That Jay and I were making it? Or that he was making it with me, not you?"

"That isn't even worth answering," I whispered when I could speak.

"Suit yourself. I knew I shouldn't have said anything." Sophie stood up. "I'd better go."

"No, wait." I'd pushed Sophie into confiding. Serena had wanted me to make her confide. Jay was right about one thing, wasn't he? I was the most dependable person in the family who was on tap here. Except Serena.

This was something we weren't going to take to Serena. Not unless, or until, we had to.

"Sit down," I heard a voice like Serena's order Sophie. It was my voice. "Have you seen a doctor?" I knew the answer before Sophie shook her head. "Then the first thing is for you to see one and find out for sure."

"Not here!" Sophie said in alarm.

"No, not here." My mind was racing. "Gran said we could have the van drive us to Pittsburgh for shopping last Saturday, remember? We didn't do it on account of the shopping you and I did at the mall. I'll tell Gran we do need to go, this week." I didn't tell her the idea of driving in the city myself panicked me. "The van can drop us at a department store and then we'll look up a—a clinic or something, in the Yellow Pages."

"We can't take Beth," Sophie said flatly.

"No." Beth was too young and too preoccupied to have this dumped on her. "Just you and me. Nobody needs to know, unless it turns out you are. And then . . ." That was as far as I could cope with. My voice trailed off.

"And then," Sophie said, "it's up to me. This is my

problem. I may be a selfish beast in a lot of ways, but I won't make you share the responsibility for those decisions."

She came over and hugged me. "You're a bit of all right, you know that? A chip off the old block. I mean that as a compliment. I'm off. No, I want to walk. I'll be fine now, don't worry. You stay here."

I stayed, closing up the now silent house and going slowly upstairs in the dark. My head was whirling. With what Sophie had told me and what she'd said just now. With Carl's words about my taking after Serena, as Sophie had just said. With what Jay had said about Serena looking for an heir apparent.

Jay. His name was like a pain in my head and in my heart.

Wise up, Sophie'd said. I was facing up to a lot of things right now. And what troubled me the most, I was ashamed to admit, wasn't Sophie's very real problem, it wasn't even the possibility of Mother having a fling.

It was Jay.

XIV

I almost called Mother just now, after Sophie left. Because what's happening is too big for me to handle. And the one person that comes to my mind is Mother.

Mother would not be shocked. She'd have plenty to say, but she would not be shocked. This is the kind of thing that she can cope with.

I got as far as looking up the international dialing code for London and picking up the receiver. And then I put it down. I'm not sure why. Well, yes, I am, but let's not go into that.

Dad? He's close. He'd come. He'd be kind, and sensible, and rational, and I'd be embarrassed. And anyway, this—mess—is Sophie's secret. Which she shared with me. So now it's my problem, too. Sophie spilled her guts to me, and I can't betray her, I can't let her down.

Dear God, what do we do now . . .?!

The phone rang the next morning before I was awake. I reached for it, thanking God and Serena for the bedroom extension, not even worrying whether it might be Mom.

It wasn't. It was Sophie, hoarse and apprehensive. "Laura? What we talked about last night—you haven't told anybody, have you?"

"In the middle of the night? How could I?"

"Thank God," Sophie breathed. "You've got to promise me you won't tell a living soul. Right now. Promise!"

I swallowed. "Don't you think you ought to tell Jay?"

"No! Maybe after I—find out. You know. I trusted you, Laura. If you blab this out, I—I don't know what I'll do. Now swear!"

I swore. I told Sophie I'd arrange for our shopping trip to Pittsburgh Saturday, and I'd find a way to keep Beth from coming. Then I went downstairs and made myself a cup of coffee. I'd run out of milk, and the brew was black and bitter, but I drank it anyway. It made me feel shaky, but wide awake. In a weird sort of way, it also put starch in my spine.

I took a bath, dressed, and looked at the clock. It was still only six-thirty A.M. Outside the windows, birds were singing, and the smell of new-mown grass floated from the green. I snapped all the shades up, and early sunlight flooded the downstairs room. A shaft struck the shelves beside the potter's wheel, and I noticed something I hadn't seen before. Gran's little urn, uncovered, was sitting on a shelf to dry for firing. Gran must have been here yesterday, some time while I was off with Jay. The little urn sat there, perfectly symmetrical, serene. I wondered what emotions Gran had poured into its symmetry.

On an impulse, I scooped some clay out of the bin and tried to center it on the wheel, but it didn't work. No matter how hard I tried, the clay went askew. Like my life, I thought, pulled in all different directions. Maybe Mom and I weren't made for symmetry.

I was getting melodramatic, and I knew it. I flung the clay back in the bin, pulled the shades down, and headed for the workshop. At least in refinishing furniture I couldn't make anything go crooked!

The workshop was locked, but like all apprentices I'd been given a key. The Shaker chair that I'd been stripping still stood where I'd left it, on my work table. I opened my can of stripper, took a clean cloth and clean metal brush, and set to work.

I don't know how long I'd been there when Carl came in. It was now three minutes after eight—I do know that. Carl came over and stood watching me for a few minutes, hands in pockets. "Making up for the time you've missed?" he asked.

"Something like that."

"I know I said you could make up time, but coming in at this hour is above and beyond the call of duty. We may be strong on commitment around here, but not on cruel and unusual punishment!" Carl bent over me to inspect the graining of the slats, and I was very conscious of his nearness.

"You do nice work, Laura," he said, straightening. "You have a real feel for old furniture, don't you?" I nodded. "I thought so. Have you ever thought of studying for museum management or restoration work in college?"

I was startled. "I've never had anything to do with old things before! At least not *good* old. Mom's a dedicated garage-sale and curbside-pickup connoisseur. But her idea of old is the nineteen fifties. And Dad's architecture is strictly modern."

"Good lines and good woods are universals, aren't they? Actually, Shaker pieces like this rocker go very well with modern," Carl said, his fingers gently stroking the cat-o'-nine-tails slat. I thought of the interior of the Potter's House and its timeless yet modern feel. Carl looked at me with a quizzical expression. "I tried to tell you some of this yesterday, but you didn't understand a word I said, did you? Museum work, or at any rate crafts work, might be perfect for you."

"Why? Because I'm Serena's granddaughter?"

"No, because you have what every truly creative

person needs if the creativity's not to be wasted: a combination of emotional involvement and rational detachment. I don't know whether that's genetic or not," Carl said as I looked at him, startled, "but certainly not all the Van Zandts have it. Serena does, and that's her real genius. And you have it. I saw it when you were coping with all the crises of festival week, and I see it in what you're doing now."

He didn't explain exactly what he was referring to, and I didn't ask.

Carl went off, whistling, and started working on some of the museum records. Nine o'clock came, and the rest of the staff arrived. I worked until noon, and then I went in search of Gran. I found her on the green opposite the church, supervising the planting of a garden.

"Laura! Come have a look at this." Gran was holding a big-brimmed garden hat on her head with one hand. She held the garden plans out to me with the other. "We're taking a chance on planting in spite of the heat. I do want the perennials well established by the fall. The rector and I are planning a harvest festival, and if the weather cooperates, we'll hold it here. What do you think?"

"It's lovely, Gran,"

She was planting a garden of biblical herbs and flowers, to balance the Shakespearean garden already obediently flowering at the other end of the green. "It will be a meditation garden," Gran said radiantly. "A church without walls, for people of all faiths. See the circular shape? That represents infinity. There will be gravel paths, and a pool with a fountain in the center. Water's a universal symbol. And benches. For now we'll make do with stones." Gran seated herself on a boulder and rummaged inside her giant straw basket for a neatly tied package. "Lunch. Smoked turkey sandwiches and strawberries. Will you join me, Laura?"

We shared the lunch box companionably. Gran asked me if I'd heard any more from my mother, and I answered evasively that I hadn't talked to her. Gran told me how much Great-Aunt Alexandra had liked the dresses Jay and I had bought. I told Gran that Sophie and I wanted to take up her offer of a van ride to Pittsburgh for more shopping. "Saturday morning. And Gran, can you find a way to keep Beth from coming with us? She doesn't really need clothes—not after the two suitcases full of them that Aunt Lisa shipped here. Sophie and I want to do a lot of tramping around, and honestly I don't think Beth can keep up with us."

Gran wanted to know why not, and I told her about Beth's ankle. Gran frowned. "I'll speak to Madame about whether Beth should see a doctor."

"What I think Beth really needs is less of Madame. Three classes a day and practice on her own besides? Gran, Madame's awfully tough."

"Not more so than the head of any world-class dance

company. Beth must understand the demands of her chosen career, and now's the time for her to come to terms with them. But you're right. It would be better if Beth did not go with you Saturday," Gran said. I learned later that Gran commanded Beth's presence at lunch on Saturday. It was an invitation Beth didn't dare refuse.

"She's got somebody from the New York City Ballet coming, so Madame will be there, too. But at least that means afternoon class will be canceled," Beth told me that night at supper.

"How's the ankle?"

"Forget my ankle. I'm tired of hearing about it," Beth said irritably. "How come Sophie's not eating with us? Has she got a date?"

"I'm not sure what she's doing," I said vaguely.

Gran's lunch party meant there wasn't any chance she'd take it into her head to drive Sophie and me on our shopping trip herself. That thought had occurred to me late and uneasily. The driver turned out to be one of the gardeners, who'd been given a list of purchases to make in Pittsburgh and regarded us as excess baggage. He dropped us in the center of Pittsburgh's Golden Triangle and told us to be waiting in front of the PPG building at exactly four o'clock. "And don't be late. I don't want to get caught in commuter traffic."

Sophie and I made for the nearest hotel that had private telephone booths and Yellow Pages. Sophie flipped through the book and then looked at me help-lessly. "I don't know what to look under." So I looked, under clinics and prenatal counseling, and found a clinic connected with one of the noted Pittsburgh hospitals. I called and found out what hours they were open and that an appointment wasn't necessary.

I flagged a cab, got Sophie and me into it, and gave the driver the address.

I sat with Sophie on the leatherette banquettes of the bright, cheerfully impersonal hospital corridor for what seemed an eternity but was only little more than an hour. This was after helping Sophie fill in lots of forms, because by now Sophie, the sophisticated world traveler, had about as much spine to her as a jellyfish.

I waited again, while Sophie was sent in to see the doctor without me. I caught a glimpse of her for a minute, in one of those awful pale green hospital gowns, following a nurse from one cubbyhole room to an-other. It was a good while before Sophie returned, in her own clothes again, looking shaky but resolute.

"It will take a few days before I know the results. They'll call me." Sophie grimaced. "One of the advan-tages of running a switchboard! The call will come straight to me. I told them to phone only during the hours I'd be working."

"How—how did it go?" I asked hesitantly.

"Not now. Let's get out of here. Lunch is on me."

So we took a cab to Station Square, and in the noisy

anonymity of Houlihan's, with its tongue-in-cheek *Ca-sablanca* decor, Sophie told me about her examination. At least she told me about some of it; I had a feeling she was holding back in deference to my innocence, and I was glad she did.

"They're nice people, really. I had a woman doctor. She looked like she's only about ten years older than me." Sophie pushed shrimp around her salad bowl. "She gave me a lot of stuff to read. Pamphlets and so on."

"Sophie? What are you going to do? That is, if—"

"I told you, I'm not dumping that on you. It's up to me to decide on the options."

I knew without her listing them what they were: Keep the baby, either as a single mother or get married (which Sophie'd said she wouldn't do). Put the baby up for adoption. (There were supposed to be a lot of people wanting to adopt newborns, weren't there?) Or an abortion.

I sat there in Houlihan's as the ceiling fan whirled, and a girl went chattering on about her latest guy at the next table, looking at my cousin with her eye-shadow and blusher that were like flags of pride on her drawn face, and thought how different all this was when it was personal, not a textbook case being discussed in Family Life class.

"Doesn't the—the father have a right to have some say?" I ventured.

"Maybe I don't think he deserves the right. Or that the kid deserves better than him as a father." Sophie fished in her purse for her wallet. "I've had enough—have you? Let's get out of here."

We went back to the Golden Triangle and hit the stores. Sophie bought more clothes, short skirts, and bare-midriff tops, and tight pants—things she couldn't possibly wear to work in.

Things she couldn't possibly wear if she were pregnant. Not if she had the baby.

My mind skittered away from what I was thinking.

We were back at the PPG building ten minutes early, and by the time the van, now full of garden supplies, arrived, Sophie had herself well under control. It was as if the far-out clothes she'd bought were a talisman against her fears.

We went back to Vredezucht. The driver pulled up in front of the Potter's House. A shining new Ford with Pennsylvania license plates was parked there. As I stepped out of the van, a masculine figure rose from one of the porch rockers.

It was Dad.

Dad, here in Vredezucht and looking much the same as always in his Saturday uniform of chinos and rugby shirt. I ran up the path, up the steps, into his arms.

"Where did you come from?" I demanded when we released each other. By now the van had gone on. "Why didn't you call?"

"I flew in this morning from Philadelphia," Dad answered, smiling. "I didn't call because I was afraid you might tell me not to come. You weren't exactly receptive the last time we talked, if you remember."

I blushed. "Anyway, I—I'm glad you came. I'm sorry I wasn't here."

"That's okay," Dad said comfortably. "I hunted up your grandmother, and she gave me the grand tour. Me and the visiting celebrity from the ballet. I had lunch with them, too, and with Beth and that old fossil Serena's hunted up to give Beth lessons."

I couldn't help laughing. "You'd better not let Serena hear you say that."

"I have some sense," Dad answered. "What's wrong with Beth? Not just the way she's limping. The rest of her."

So I told Dad everything I knew, including about Madame's terrorist tactics. "If Beth won't complain to Serena, you do it for her," Dad advised. "I can't believe Serena would approve."

"You'd be surprised. Under the caftan is a will of iron. What Gran accomplishes is wonderful, but . . . I don't know. When dedication to a vision is that strong, there's almost a—a ruthlessness about it." I stopped abruptly.

"About your mother," Dad said, as if he'd read my mind, "have you talked to her?"

"No, I don't want to." I didn't want to talk to Dad

about all that, either. At least, I thought I didn't, but before I knew it there I was, spilling my guts, and Dad sat back in the porch swing and let me talk. Afterward, Dad suggested we both shower and change and he'd take me to dinner at the Monongahela House. So I explained about the shower shortage in the Potter's House, and he went next door to use Beth's shower while I took a bath and put on my flowered voile. We had dinner in style at the Monongahela House, and Dad told me all about how his project was coming along in Philadelphia. We didn't talk about Mom at all.

Dad spent the night at the Potter's House, on the living room couch to be exact. On Sunday morning he and I went to church, and sat with Serena in the Van Zandt family pew, along with Beth and Great-Aunt Alexandra and (to my surprise) Sophie. Maybe she needed church. I certainly did. The fact that Sophie's thoughts had turned in that direction made me feel closer to her.

After church we all went back to Gran's for dinner, and of that meal and the afternoon and evening that followed, only two incidents stood out sharply clear.

The first was when Gran had dinner ready and called us to the table. Great-Aunt Alexandra had gone upstairs for a lie-down after church, and when she didn't respond to the gong, Gran sent Sophie up to fetch her. Sophie was halfway up the stairs when Great-Aunt Alexandra let out a cry.

We all ran to the hall. Great-Aunt Alexandra was on the upstairs landing, clutching the rails and shouting. "My money! My money's gone!"

Gran ran upstairs, passing Sophie with the speed of someone half her age. "Alexandra, calm down and tell us what has happened."

"My money, that's what's happened!" Great-Aunt Alexandra let herself be steered to a big chair, but her hands worked on Gran's arm and her eyes were on fire. "All my money I keep under my handkerchiefs in my bureau drawer—it's gone. This is all that's left."

She held it out. *This* was a small roll of bills. The one on the outside was a five-hundred-dollar bill.

"Alexandra, I've told you not to keep quantities of money around. It's much better off in the bank," Gran said. "You gave money to Jay and Laura to buy new dresses for you, don't you remember?"

Great Aunt-Alexandra's dark eyes fastened on Gran, bewildered. Her wrinkled hand plucked at the bosom of the new gray voile dress. At the same time, Sophie spoke, shrill and rather high.

"Great-Aunt Alexandra, you gave Jay money to buy a car with, don't you remember?"

Great-Aunt Alexandra stared at her vaguely.

"Alexandra, it's all right. I'll explain later," Gran said soothingly. "Right now Sunday dinner's on the table. We have a guest. Laura's father's here. You remember Kenneth Blair, Alexandra."

It was obvious she didn't. But it tugged at my heart

to watch Great-Aunt Alexandra respond with automatic courtesy. "Oh . . . of course, Kenneth Blair. How nice."

She came downstairs like a dowager duchess, and Dad greeted her in kind. Behind them, Sophie and I exchanged troubled glances. Jay, and the money for the car. . . . She did give it to him. She's just forgotten about it, I told myself violently. But a little worm of suspicion, however unfair, twisted in my mind.

That was one of the things I would remember. The other was the conversation Dad and I had, very late Sunday evening, on the porch. It was easier to talk in darkness, and we talked a lot. When I tried afterward to reconstruct the conversation in my journal, I couldn't chart its path. I do know I told Dad about how I was loving my work, and how Carl had said that it could be my calling. Not just refinishing, but the administrative and creative end of it. Dad told me for the first time how he'd come to decide to be an architect. And he told me about the letter he'd had from Mom.

"How can you be so darn calm about all this?" I demanded.

In the darkness, I heard him give a small laugh. "Laura, don't you be deceived the way your mother often is. A calm surface doesn't necessarily mean a lack of feeling."

"Okay, if you want me to buy that, tell me how you do it."

"I'm not sure I can. It may be natural temperament; it may be experience." Dad looked at me. "For one thing, I've known for a long time that this was coming someday. So, I think, has your mother. I think we both tried to keep you from knowing, hoping against hope . . . I don't know whether we succeeded, and whether trying to protect you was right or wrong."

I didn't answer.

"There's one good thing about waiting a long time for the second shoe to drop," Dad said conversationally. "You get used to the fact that it will. If it doesn't, that's a pleasant surprise. If it does, it's more a—a relief than anything. The waiting's over and the wondering. You know."

I thought of Sophie, waiting for the test results. "You mean it's better knowing?" I asked in a small voice.

"It's always better knowing, I think," Dad answered. "Uncertainty's what's unbearable. You imagine the most awful things."

"That the world's coming to an end," I said wryly.

"Yes. But it doesn't, you know. Only the world you're used to. Take me, for example. I still have you. I have my work, which is very important to me. I have my gifts, as your grandmother would call them, and my health, thank God. So do you, Laura. You'll always have Kay and me, even if the three of us aren't together."

And Gran, and Aunt Lisa, and Sophie, and Beth, I thought.

"From the sound of things, you have your gifts, too," Dad said. "I'm glad you're finding them. They can mean a lot."

"They can't make me understand why Mom has to go . . . chasing off like an aging hippie to find herself."

This time Dad laughed out loud. "Who on earth is that a quote from? Surely not Serena. It sounds more like your Aunt Rena, and she's certainly in no position to throw stones."

"You don't know the half of that," I said darkly.

"I'd just as soon not," Dad agreed. "Seriously, though, Laura, one of the reasons I can be so calm, as you call it, is because I do understand Kay's needs. Maybe that's what she can't take about me, the fact that I understood them better than she did herself. Painful as it is in a lot of ways, I do know that it was right for Kay to go to England."

"How can you know what's right for you? What you need?" I burst out. "Particularly if you have a lot of responsibilities? Or a lot of gifts? When one thing conflicts with another . . . or with what other people want or need." I was thinking now of Sophie and my vow of silence. "How can you know what's right?"

Dad was silent for a moment. "I think what's right is what gives you peace," he said at last. "And joy. I'm not talking about happiness or kicks. And I'm not talking about absence of tension. I'm talking about the peace in the eye of the hurricane. I knew a guy once who used to fly one of those weather planes. He said it was hell going through a storm's turbulence, but once you got in its eye, the air was absolutely calm, despite the turbulence around you. That's what I mean. And I'm also not talking about the joy of finishing something, or getting something. I mean the harmony in the act of doing."

I had sudden vivid pictures of Gran at the potter's wheel, of myself working on the Shaker rocker. But then the picture of my mother rose, and I shut my mind. Dad was wrong. All that—philosophy—didn't apply, not to Mother's walking out on Dad and me.

XV

⟪✸⟫ *Journal—July 18*

I got a letter from Mother today. It started out, "Oh, sweetie, I do know how you feel. I really do understand. I hope you'll be fair enough to realize how I feel, too—"

That's as far as I got. Then *I got the shakes, and I ran next door to Beth and told her to read the darn thing and tell me what I needed to know. Beth gave me one of those looks of hers, but she did it. There wasn't anything in the letter that was new.*

I keep remembering a line from The Crucible *that we read in English: "There are wheels within wheels in this village, and fires within fires." That's what I'm feeling like now. There's wheels within wheels in Vredezucht. At first I thought it was all so beautiful. My place of peace. Now I'm seeing beneath the surface, and I hate it. Beth's bruises. Gran's iron hand. Dad being so calm, instead of fighting to make Mom come back. Sophie's mess. Jay. Great-Aunt Alexandra.*

Great-Aunt Alexandra. She's like a beautiful old fig-urine that's crumbling to pieces while we watch. I hate to say it, but she's gotten worse just since I've been here.

I hate to say it, but maybe she didn't forget about giving Jay the money for the car. I hate to think it, but I wouldn't put it past him to—no, I can't even write that.

That week while we waited for the test results was the worst one of my life. Not just because of Sophie's mess—that's what I kept on calling it, "Sophie's mess," skittering away from the real, blunt words. But because the . . . the maybe-baby seemed to symbolize all the wheels within wheels. Situations that could have been foreseen. Situations rushed into, heedlessly, on the strong winds of passions and emotions. Situations developing unwanted, unanticipated . . . and yet when you look back, you can see how the circumstances that created them started long before. Like the chain of Marley's Ghost, forged link by link. By things done and things not done.

I'm getting so darned literary lately. My English teacher would be pleased. It's a hell of a lot easier to deal with things in literary terms than in real life.

And so we waited for the second shoe to drop.

Dad flew back to Milwaukee early Monday morning, to spend what he hoped would be "a couple of unin-terrupted weeks at the home office." Then he'd have to come to Philadelphia again. He wanted me to visit him there. I said I would. He wanted me to at least write to Mother. I said I'd think about it.

On Monday morning, Gran phoned the workshop and asked if I could meet her for lunch. Monongahela House. Her treat. I knew what was coming, but I figured in a public restaurant she wouldn't be able to get too personal. I underestimated my Serena. In the most gracious and most oblique way, using phrases nobody at the nearby tables would understand but I did full well, she proceeded to cross-examine me on my father.

How did I think he was? He seemed quite satisfied in spite of everything with how the Philadelphia project was progressing; did I agree? Had he said anything about going abroad himself?

"Really, Gran! Why didn't you ask him yourself?" I blurted out at last.

Gran's eyebrows rose delicately. "Laura, really! I didn't want to trouble him. I know the situation disturbs you as much as it does me, but I thought you were mature enough now for us to discuss the situation rationally."

"I'm sorry, but I don't feel rational about it."

Gran devoted herself to her chicken salad for a while, and then talked about the meditation garden. She was very pleased with the plants the gardener had brought back from Pittsburgh. "And how did your shopping expedition go?" she asked casually. I shot a quick glance at her, but her face was calm.

"It was okay. Sophie bought a lot of stuff, but I don't think you're going to be too pleased if she wears them to the office."

"I'm just pleased that Sophie's here this summer, that all three of you are," Gran said. "I've heard wonderful things about your work from Carl. And Beth's dancing's making a bit of progress, Madame tells me."

"I suppose so."

I was being abrupt, but I was afraid if I wasn't I'd say something that I shouldn't. Fortunately, Gran didn't seem to notice.

"It really made me so happy, having all the family here for my birthday and the dedication. If only Kay could have made it, too—but of course, this writing assignment's such a wonderful opportunity for her at last. When you write her, Laura, please tell her I really do understand." That could have meant a lot of things, including a fishing expedition to find out whether Mom and I were corresponding. I didn't say anything, and Gran kept on talking. "Family reunions can seem pretty dry and stuffy when you're young, I know. But as one gets older . . . I knew," Gran said, carefully straightening the silverware, "this June might be the last chance we'd have to be all together."

I was surprised to see tears sparkling in her eyes. "Gran," I said uncomfortably. Gran's hand, the one with the big amethyst ring, came up.

"No. Please. There's something I have to ask you,

and I need a straight answer, please. About Alexandra. To the best of your knowledge, did she give Jay money to buy a car?"

"I don't know," I said after a long pause.

When the red mist of anger receded from my eyes, Gran was looking at me with grave compassion. "I was going to ask you what you thought," she said. "But I won't." I had a feeling it was because she didn't have to.

"I almost forgot to tell you," she said with a complete change of subject. "We're going to have a real treat at the Opera House a week from Saturday. My friend from the New York City Ballet, whom you and Sophie missed meeting because you were in Pittsburgh—he and his partner will be coming through Pennsylvania on their way to an engagement in Indiana. They've agreed to give a recital, a benefit for the study center. I shall have to get busy with publicity and lining up the rest of the program. Perhaps the chamber music quartet will play again. Now do let's have some dessert."

I had a darn good suspicion where Gran's thoughts were leading, and so did Beth when I told her about our conversation, while we were swimming in the river before dinner.

"I'm not going to get up there and make a fool of myself!" Beth exploded. "Not in front of him! He's too good!"

"Calm down," Sophie said. "The Queen wouldn't push you if she didn't think you were good, too."

"She won't if she talks to Madame," Beth said darkly.

"Another run-in?" I asked apprehensively.

"Don't ask."

I started wondering whether I should call Aunt Lisa and tell her to come to her daughter's rescue. Then I thought: It can wait.

Some of the other apprentices were swimming, too, and they suggested hitting the highway for hamburgers. Sophie and Beth and I went along. When I got home, it was after dark, and there was an overnight letter from Mother waiting for me.

So help me, the first thing that crossed my mind was whether Gran had known about it, whether she'd thought I might have already read it. The second was that at least she hadn't phoned. The third was that Dad and Gran were right: I did owe it to my mother to hear her side.

I opened the letter, and I started reading, and before I reached the second paragraph I felt as if I were coming down with the flu. Mom's writing was so slapdash, so familiar, so like the millions of letters and cards and door-of-the-refrigerator notes back through the years. I couldn't go on. I took it to Beth and had her summarize.

Beth read it in silence. "There's one thing important. She says she won't phone you again, not till you call her. So you can stop being afraid to answer the phone."

"How's her . . . work going?"

"Good. There's a lot about interviews she's had, and a book-and-author luncheon. And a couple of publisher's parties. She's been meeting a lot of interesting people."

"So at least her social life's improving," I said snidely.

Beth just looked at me. "If you mean is she seeing anybody, she does mention that one guy from the publisher quite a lot. But not in any way special. I don't think you have to worry."

"I'm not . . . worrying," I said at last, with difficulty. "It's just . . . everything's changing so, so fast."

"Maybe it's not really fast," Beth said, as if she'd known what I'd been thinking earlier. "Maybe everything's been building up for a long time beneath the surface, and we're just starting to realize it."

"We?"

"You're not the only person things like that happen to, you know," Beth said ambiguously.

"Don't I know it. . . . Beth, can I ask you something?"

"You can ask." Beth's face was pale.

"How would you feel if Aunt Lisa—if she got serious about somebody?"

Clearly that was not what Beth had been expecting. "I'd like it," she said at last. "After Dad died, for a while I wished she would. Of course, that's different," she added as she saw my face. "After a while, I got used to things the way they are. But I'd like her to be happy. I'd like her to have somebody besides me. It could be . . . easier."

"I suppose you're right," I said thoughtfully. "Maybe for Dad, too. Someday." It was a thought that had not occurred to me before. "But not for a while. Right now I—I feel like every darn vase I've tried to throw on the potter's wheel. They may start out right, but all of a sudden they're off-center. That's what I feel like now."

To my shame, I felt tears gathering in my eyes. "I know I've been what Sophie would call a 'selfish beast.' About Mom, I mean." I fingered the envelope, but did not take the letter out. "It's just . . . I can't see straight. Everything's out of focus. Nothing's fixed and certain."

Beth said a surprising thing. " 'Things most surely believed.' " It was a quote from something—I didn't know what—that I'd heard at church a lot. "I guess whenever the fixed certain thing in our lives changes, everything else changes, too."

Me, and Mom, and Dad. Nuclear family. That had been my fixed constant. Only it wasn't going to be that way again. Not ever. Dad hadn't said so, Mom hadn't said so—but I knew.

That was Monday. On Tuesday, Gran informed Madame that Beth should have a dance piece prepared to present at the benefit performance a week from Saturday. Madame informed Beth of this at her afternoon class, together with a lot of additional remarks about what an honor and a privilege Beth was receiving and how the least she could do was strive to be more worthy. The implication being that Beth certainly was *not*.

"I'll bet she didn't come out with any of that in front of Gran," I snorted when Beth told me.

"Maybe she should have," Beth said. "Because she's right."

So that's what's bothering Beth, I thought, illumined. She's afraid she can't be good enough. Not just now: ever. And Beth, like Gran, was a perfectionist.

On Wednesday I got a postcard from Jay, who was on the coast of Maine, of all places: "Having marvelous time. Wish you were here. Car performing splendidly. First dent now in place! Love, Jay." Not a word about Sophie, or Great-Aunt Alexandra, and neither of them heard from him. I knew, because I checked.

"Don't you think you ought to talk to him?" I asked Sophie seriously.

"I told you, no. The hell with him," Sophie said, chain-smoking. She shot me a look. "Tell the truth. What do you think's the real story about Great-Aunt Alexandra's bankroll and that car?"

"I can't believe Jay just took the money," I said carefully.

"Oh, I can. I can also believe Great-Aunt A. said or did something to give him the idea it was quite all

right. She's going batty, and he's a charming con-man."
Sophie blew out smoke. "I don't mean he's a thief! If
he did help himself, he'd be sure it was an okay thing—
because she'd promised and forgotten, because she's
loaded and didn't need it, because she'd promised him,
'Everything I have will be yours.' You name it. Just
because he's my cousin doesn't mean I don't see through
him, and if you hadn't been so naive you would have,
too."

"Then why . . . " I faltered, reddening.

"Oh, for Pete's sake, Laura! Grow up!"

Wednesday was also Beth's night to cook for the
weekly "family dinner." She had Gran and Sophie and
me come to Wisteria Cottage for fettucine Alfredo (it
was good) and salad, and she was very quiet. Gran
talked mostly about the upcoming benefit.

Thursday was the day the local weekly paper came
out, and it carried a large announcement of the benefit.
Sophie's switchboard became busy, for the Pittsburgh
papers carried the announcement, too, and so did *The
New York Times*. The local chamber music quartet had
been corralled and was rehearsing. Madame was crack-
ing the whip over Beth. I finished my work on the
Shaker rocker, and started on another piece, a Pembroke table. All this was going on, and somehow it
wasn't reaching me. I was going through the motions,
but the *I* of me was somewhere else. Not in the eye of
that hurricane Dad had spoken of, more like in limbo.

I, like Sophie, was waiting for the shoe to drop.

I never asked Sophie whether she'd heard the test results; I knew she'd tell me. Neither Sophie nor I mentioned that Pittsburgh trip at all.

Late Friday morning Sophie phoned me at the workshop. "Come for lunch at my digs. Half past twelve." She hung up.

By half past twelve my stomach was tied in knots. I walked up the outside stairs to Sophie's small apartment, and Sophie was standing in the doorway waiting. She pulled me inside and hugged me hard. "It's okay. The clinic phoned. I'm *not*."

"Sophie, I'm so glad."

"How do you think I feel?" Sophie released me. Behind her makeup her face was pale, but her eyes looked relieved. "I guess I just pushed the panic button too soon. I've always been a weirdo when it came to being on regular schedules, biologically speaking as well as otherwise. So when I started feeling whoopsy all the time, when I looked at food and even when I didn't . . ." She took a deep breath. "The doc says it wasn't morning sickness, it was some kind of exotic bug I picked up. Probably from some of the exotic food Jay and I ate in those cheap London restaurants."

"So how come Jay didn't get it, too?" I couldn't help asking.

"Jay," Sophie said, "leads a charmed life." She set out bread and cheese. "You know something funny?"

she asked at last. "I was almost getting to like the idea of having a kid. Not now, but someday. After the messes Mummy and I have managed to make of our lives, I'd always figured it wouldn't be fair for a kid to have me as a mum. Now I'm not so sure."

We sat down to what Sophie called a "plowman's lunch"—sharp Cheddar cheese and crusty bread, pickled onions and chutney. "I finally feel like eating again," Sophie said.

"Sophie, what *were* you going to do?" I asked presently.

"If the test had been positive, you mean? No way, José. Whatever I said, it'd make you feel bad. And responsible. You've taken enough responsibility for me already. I don't know what I'd have done without you this summer—I mean that," Sophie said fervently. And then, as if betrayed into sentimentality, she added, "Have some more cider."

XVI

*The Van Zandt Foundation
requests the pleasure of your company
at a special performance
for the benefit of
The Van Zandt Institute of Arts and Letters,
Mikhail Takalevsky and Diane ver Veyl, guest soloists,
at the Opera House
Saturday afternoon, the thirtieth of July,
at two-thirty p.m.
Reception on the River Terrace to follow*

So the other shoe had dropped. Or rather, there wasn't a shoe to drop at all.

Dad phoned Friday night and said he had to be back in Philadelphia after all, and why didn't I join him for the weekend. Gran could have somebody drive me to the Pittsburgh airport Saturday morning. "Don't you drive there! I got a good look at your mother's old car while I was there last weekend, and I don't want you driving it on highways any more till it's overhauled." And Dad would meet me.

I was feeling guilty about the time I'd missed from work in the past few weeks—I'd gotten back from lunch late on Friday, too—and I'd meant to put in some weekend hours at the workshop. I hesitated a good thirty seconds and said yes anyway. I had a feeling that I needed not just to be with Dad, but to get away from Vredezucht for a while.

Philadelphia was fun. I'd never spent much time with Dad alone before, and I liked it. We stayed at the Four Seasons, which was very fancy. During the day on Saturday we visited Independence Hall, the Liberty Bell, and the Betsy Ross House. We had dinner at the hotel, where there was dinner dancing. I wore the dress he'd bought me, and we danced. I felt—as I had been feeling a good deal lately—as though I'd entered into a different world.

On Sunday Dad and I went to church, had brunch, and visited the art museum. And Dad drove me to see the shopping mall that he'd designed. Some of what I'd been learning from Carl must have rubbed off on me; I could see a correlation between the mall design and the buildings around Rittenhouse Square, and Dad was pleased.

"That's exactly what I was trying to do, capture the

proportions and spatial relationships of the colonial city, but in modern design. That was very astute of you, Laura."

"I can't take the credit. I've been learning a lot this summer. From Gran and from Carl Lindstrom."

That led to a lot of talk about my workshop work, and Carl, and his ambitions. "I want to meet him, next time I come there," Dad said. "It sounds as if you're really at home in Vredezucht, Laura."

"I guess I am," I answered, surprised.

"Would you want to stay there? No, don't answer right away. But sometime during the next few weeks we'll have to make plans. It looks as if I'll be going back and forth between Elm Grove and Philadelphia for the next eight months at least. Equal time in each place, or even more in Philadelphia. I don't want you living alone part of the time, trying to keep house while you go to school." Dad didn't say anything about Mother's possibly returning, and I didn't either. "You could stay in Vredezucht and go to school there; I'm sure your grandmother would be willing. Or I could get a live-in housekeeper in Elm Grove. Or here in Philadelphia, if you want to come here."

"I don't know," I said slowly.

"Think about it, and we'll talk in a week or so," Dad said. "By the way, how's Beth doing?"

So I told him what I'd deduced, about Beth being afraid she couldn't live up to everyone's expectations.

Dad smiled wryly. "Sounds like your mother, except that Beth truly wants to! Try to get her to see it's not necessary to be the *prima ballerina assoluta* of the world, can't you?"

"You try. You know the family ethic. 'If a thing's worth doing, it's worth doing perfectly.' "

"There's no such thing as absolute perfection. Serena knows that, even if her family thinks she doesn't. Now shut up and eat your peach Melba," Dad said and grinned.

I remembered that conversation when Gran showed up to put some time in at the potter's wheel Sunday evening. She asked if I'd gotten any handle on what was bothering Beth, and I told her. She nodded thoughtfully. "You may be right. I have to admit, Madame Karhanova is chary with the compliments. She belongs to the old school; compliments make students complacent, only continual correction leads to improvement."

"Continual nagging, you mean."

"Then the rest of us must be sure to offer Beth more encouragement," Gran said. "Now what about Sophie? She's settling in better, isn't she?"

I told Gran truthfully that nothing in the world was bothering Sophie. And I got her off the subject of family and onto the benefit, before she could do any probing about Dad and Mother.

July was drawing to a close. I'd been in Vredezucht

almost five weeks, I realized, startled. Mother'd been in England even longer. It seemed only days, yet it seemed a lifetime.

That last week of July, the benefit performance occupied everybody's mind. Gran, remembering the Living Picture show, decided I should coordinate arrangements for the visiting dignitaries since her secretary was on vacation and I was "turning out to be so gifted at management."

"And how she came to that conclusion after all the things that went wrong with those darn performances, I do not know!" I groaned to Carl. This was on Tuesday evening, while I was putting in some overtime on the Pembroke table and working out arrangements with him at the same time.

Carl laughed. "Don't put yourself down. You do have a gift for it; you're simply inexperienced, which time will cure. The question isn't what went wrong with the picture show, but how well you coped. Cousins copping out or passing out weren't your fault."

"I just hope Beth doesn't pass out again. She's pushing too hard."

"Then stop her. Or stop things for her," Carl said calmly. He looked at the table leg I'd been working on. "You have a lot of talents, Laura Serena Blair, and don't let anyone convince you otherwise. Now let's knock off work and go get some ice cream."

"I've got some in my freezer. Why don't you come over to the Potter's House and have it?" I asked on impulse. So Carl drove me home, and we made root beer floats with vanilla fudge ice cream, and ate them on the front porch, companionably rocking.

"The peepers are out already. End of summer's coming," Carl said. "I'll be back in grad school before I know it. What will you be doing?"

I told him about my conversation with Dad, and that led to my telling him about our sightseeing, and Dad's mall, and the comparison I'd made. Carl, too, was pleased. "See, you have learned a lot."

"Thanks to you."

"And to your own good eye. And brain. Next time I'm in Philadelphia, I'll have to have a look at that mall. Or if you're there, maybe you can show me around. If you do decide to move to Philadelphia, why don't you take some courses at the museum or the fine arts center?"

"I'll think about it."

Across the green, the clock in the church steeple struck eleven. Carl rose. "I had no idea it was so late." He walked to the steps, and I walked with him. We stood for a moment, smiling at each other. "I guess by now I can tell you," Carl said, "I was pretty ticked off when Serena said I'd have to add a green kid onto my group of carefully chosen apprentices. I was wrong. You're not so green, and I should have known that, seeing as Serena said you could hack it. And you're not really a kid."

He bent and kissed me lightly.

It was only a moment, not even a minute, but in those seconds something changed, and we both knew it. Carl went down the steps without looking back, and I heard him whistling faintly as he got into his car. And as I went into the house my heart was pounding.

I thought about what Carl had said, about stopping Beth. Okay, I'll be honest—thinking about that was less discombobulating than thinking about that kiss. Only I never got to put my two cents' worth in, because before I could, Beth—or Beth's ankle, rather—did it for me. I went over to the Opera House after work on Wednesday, intending to scoop her up and cart her somewhere for a serious talk before we ate the dinner at Gran's that Sophie was preparing. ("Fish and chips, luvs, and never you mind if it comes from the supermarket freezer, just don't tell her.") I got there while Madame was still working Beth over, and I watched through the door's glass window.

The stereo was blaring, and Madame was thumping away on the floor with her stick, flailing it at times in Beth's direction. I couldn't hear what she was saying, but I could see what Beth was doing. Beth bit her lip, and wiped her forehead, and went back to her place near the far corner and went into what she called a "preparation." Then she launched herself into space, and came down, hard, sideways on the foot with the bad ankle. The foot doubled beneath her, and the ankle gave way, and Beth was on the floor.

She was so still I'd have thought she was unconscious if it hadn't been for the agony in her face.

I didn't need Carl's voice in my head, telling me what to do. Instantly I was wrenching the door open, running inside, shouting to Madame to go get help, get Gran. I literally threw her out, and then I ran to the nearest john, and yanked off my own blouse and soaked it in water, and ran back to Beth. She was holding her ankle now, and moaning. The ankle was twice its normal size.

I bathed her face, then wrapped my sopping blouse around her ankle. "It's okay, help's coming. Hang onto me."

Beth's fingernails dug into my arm. "Remember your promise—"

"Beth, you've *got* to tell Gran now—"

"No! *Promise* . . ."

So again I promised, because I was afraid of the effect on Beth if I didn't.

Beth hung onto me all the way to the doctor's office, in the van, with Carl at the wheel and Gran sitting beside us anxiously. The doctor had a lot of things to say about stupid girls trying to push themselves too far for darn fool shows. He took X rays and bound Beth's ankle with an elastic bandage, and looked Gran and me straight in the eyes.

"She's retorn the same ligament she tore before. I'll not answer for the consequences if she puts her weight on that leg again. Keep her off it for at least two weeks, understand?"

Gran wanted to take Beth home with her, but Beth was so adamant that Gran gave in for fear of upsetting her more. We took Beth back to Wisteria Cottage. Carl carried her up to her room, and I put her to bed after throwing both him and my grandmother out of the house. Gran, to my astonishment, went docilely. Carl gave me a look of mixed amusement and admiration as he left.

I went back upstairs and announced to Beth that I was moving in. "For the duration, or at least for the next few days."

"At least now I don't have to dance in that darn benefit," Beth said irrelevantly.

So the weekly family dinner did not take place that night. Sophie duly served Gran fish and chips, as scheduled, and afterward she brought the leftovers to us. "Not wrapped in newspapers like they ought to be; Gran wouldn't let me. But they're not too bad, so dig in, chums." She was wearing one of the outrageous outfits she'd bought in Pittsburgh, and her hair was again tricolored.

"For me own morale. I'll wash it out before work tomorrow, but five weeks was all I could stand of being prim and proper. Me! My word!" She was in an exuberant mood, for the first time with no dark shadows under it, and we all had a good time, even Beth.

On Thursday and Friday I divided my time between sitting with Beth, working on the Pembroke table, and being Gran's appointed "administrator" of the gala. Takalevsky and ver Veyl were arriving on Friday and had requested housing where they would not be disturbed. Gran was putting them in the house where Aunt Rena'd stayed. I went over and made up the beds. I arranged with the chef at the hotel to have a light lunch delivered to them Saturday at the Opera House, where they would be rehearsing. I arranged for the dinner he was catering at Gran's house on Saturday, after the reception. "Just choose what you think best. I trust you," Gran had said to me with one of those vague radiant glances.

Sophie was a big help. "Least I can do for you," she said cheerfully and stayed at the switchboard through lunchtime and after hours, answering out-of-town requests for information and fending off celebrity seekers with surprising tact.

I hadn't heard Sophie in that good shape for ages, I thought happily, putting down the phone after having Sophie assure me that she'd take care of sending a limo to the airport for the VIPs, "and never you worry, ducks." Certainly not since we'd arrived in Vredezucht. Not even when she'd phoned me back in Elm Grove—

Not even when she'd phoned me back in Elm Grove. Weeks before coming to the States. She'd phoned, sounding like a basket case, needing my mom, after she'd decamped from boarding school on the trail of her rock singer. She hadn't found him, and she'd parked herself on Jay instead. Whom she'd just met. When she was already a jittery wreck.

The truth hit me like a bullet, right between the eyes. She'd already suspected she was pregnant then. Way back then. Which meant Jay couldn't have been the father. Okay, I thought harshly, so she and Jay probably had been making it anyway. But she knew the maybe-baby couldn't be Jay's. That's why she wouldn't tell him.

She'd told me he was. No, wait a minute. She'd made me think it and hadn't contradicted.

I was so angry I didn't trust myself to be near Sophie. The anger built and built through Friday. Sophie tracked me down by phone—Gran wanted to know whether I'd come over to help her welcome the VIPs. "I'm too busy," I said shortly.

"Laura?" Sophie asked. "Are you okay?"

"Just busy. Make up a story for Gran, will you? You're good at it." I hung up, to find Carl looking at me quizzically.

"Just last-minute tension," I said lightly, but I had a feeling I hadn't fooled him.

I went to the Opera House after work to check on arrangements, and to the Monongahela House for the same reason. When I reached Wisteria Cottage, I found Sophie there, plying Beth with hamburgers and gossip.

"I was going to cook," I said shortly.

I saw Beth and Sophie exchange glances. "Okay, we know you're superwoman. Save it for somebody you can impress," Sophie said soothingly. "Have a hamburger." I ate and calmed down, but I didn't get off that easily. When I went downstairs for iced tea, Sophie followed. "Spit it out. What's eating you?" she demanded.

I looked her straight in the eyes. "You thought you were pregnant when you ran away from school, didn't you? That's why you were looking for your rocker! You knew all along that Jay couldn't be the father!"

"So maybe I did," Sophie said at last, steadily. "Jay and I were making it, you know."

"I don't want to hear about it!"

"Maybe that's why I told you," Sophie said. "Maybe that's why I let you think what you did. You're such a darn baby, in some ways, and you're my pal, and I didn't want you to get hurt. I didn't want Jay to lead you on and dump you the way that other rat did me. If I'd tried to warn you about Jay, would you have believed me?"

Sophie was right. I wouldn't.

I looked at her, and to my disgust I started to cry, and then Sophie got teary, too. We hugged each other, and then it dawned on us that Beth would start wondering what was going on, so we wiped our eyes and took the iced tea upstairs.

Beth couldn't dance in the benefit, but that didn't mean she missed it. Gran sent the van for her, and Carl carried her down to it, carefully. She sat in a wheelchair, near the front of the auditorium, and Sophie and I sat with her. Takalevsky and ver Veyl danced beautifully, and Beth got quieter and quieter. Afterward, at the reception, Gran made a point of bringing the dancers over so Beth could meet them, and said a lot of encouraging things about Beth's talent.

Ver Veyl commiserated over Beth's ankle and told tales of her own injuries, and Takalevsky said he hoped Beth would soon audition for his company, and Beth kept on getting quieter. The reception ended and the dancers, the members of the quartet, a few selected guests, and Sophie and I went to Gran's for dinner. Beth was supposed to, but she begged off, her face strained, and she wouldn't let me go home with her. So Carl drove off with her, with Sophie in the van to see Beth safe to bed, and I went with Gran and the guests to Gran's house where Sophie'd join us later.

That was why Sophie and Beth missed what happened.

We arrived back at Gran's house at twilight. The caterers from the hotel were already there and had lit the lamps and candles. We went into the lower hall. I remember Takalevsky and ver Veyl standing there, exclaiming over the house's beauty. I think Takalevsky had just spotted the Fabergé piece on the hall table.

And then Great-Aunt Alexandra came out on the

upstairs landing. She stood there for a minute as if preparing for an entrance, and then she started down the stairs. I heard one of the musicians, behind me, murmur, "My lord, it's the mad scene from *Lucia*."

Great-Aunt Alexandra had on the black lace gown, with the train, that she'd worn for Gran's birthday dinner. Only she hadn't remembered to put a slip on under it. You could see her pink old-lady's underpants and the ribs in her scrawny chest. She had her diamond tiara on, and lots of rings, and her hand was extended for gentlemen to kiss.

"Good evening, good evening . . . I am the Dowager Countess von Hohenlohe. . . . Good evening. . . . Ah, Serena, my dear, I'm distressed to tell you, but my diamond necklace has disappeared. A thief must have broken in."

"I put it in the safe-deposit box after the Fourth of July," Gran said very quietly. Everybody was very quiet. I looked at Gran. For the first time ever she looked old. There were tears in her eyes and wrinkles around them, and she just stood there helplessly. And I knew what I must do.

I went up the stairs and linked my arm through my great-aunt's. "Great-Aunt Alexandra, it's Laura. Come upstairs with me, please. I need your help. Your—" I swallowed hard and dropped my voice to a stage whisper. "Your tiara needs adjusting. And I'll find a necklace for you to wear."

Great-Aunt Alexandra hesitated. Then she flashed

the ghost of Jay's charming smile. "My niece needs me. I will return presently," she informed the room at large and let me guide her up the stairs.

I got her into her room, and into a long black slip and then the dress again. I redid her hair and anchored the tiara on it securely. And I rummaged in Gran's own jewelry chest till I found a necklace large and glittery enough to satisfy her. Then I took her downstairs again. God bless good manners. Not one person at that large dining table indicated by word or glance that anything had gone wrong. And they all treated Great-Aunt Alexandra as if she were young and beautiful.

At last, blessedly, they were all gone. "I believe I will retire now. I am very tired," Great-Aunt Alexandra said grandly and trailed up the stairs. Sophie, who'd caught on that she'd missed a fiasco and had sneaked into the kitchen to be filled in by the hired help, went with her. Gran and I were left alone together in the downstairs hall.

"Please come inside a moment," Gran said unevenly, and led the way into her study and shut the door. She turned to me, and I saw that she was trembling.

"All I can say is thank you. I stood there—I couldn't do anything—and you handled it beautifully. I'm very, very proud of you and so grateful."

"I just did what had to be done," I said gruffly.

"You saw the need and filled it. Instantly. Graciously. I don't know what happened to me, but I . . ."

Gran groped her way to a chair and sank down in it. "I just cannot bear what's happening to Alexandra."

"Gran? What are you going to do about it?"

"I don't know," Gran said starkly, and that was the greatest shock of all.

"I'll have to do something," she said at last. "But I hate to. It's so humiliating for Alexandra. I suppose I had better send for Roger."

"Jay's closer. He's her great-grandson."

"Jay doesn't have the brains he was born with, and even less empathy," Gran said with a flash of her old vigor. "There's no way in the world I'd trust anyone's future to him. But oh, my dear, there are no easy answers."

Her head dropped on her hand.

I went and hugged her. "Get some sleep. I'm sleeping over with Beth, so there'll be nobody in the Potter's House if you want to use the wheel for a while in the morning," I whispered. I kissed the top of her head and tiptoed out.

XVII

 Journal—Saturday, July 31

To every thing there is a season,
  and a time to every purpose under the heaven.
A time to be born, and a time to die;
  a time to plant, and a time
    to pluck up that which is planted;

A time to kill, and a time to heal;
  A time to break down, and a time to build up;
A time to weep, and a time to laugh;
  A time to mourn, and a time to dance . . .
A time to get, and a time to lose;
  A time to keep, and a time to cast away. . . .

ECCLESIASTES 3:1–4, 6

August came. Already the days were growing shorter. Heat lay over Vredezucht like a still, heavy blanket. But beneath the surface, winds of change were in the air.

One change, the most noticeable change, was Great-Aunt Alexandra. Nobody was pretending any more that she wasn't senile. "Alzheimer's disease, do you think?" Sophie asked me, and I frowned.

"I don't know. All forgetfulness isn't Alzheimer's."

"It's not just forgetfulness, and you know it," Sophie said. She went over and stirred up the fire. It was Saturday, a week after the benefit, and raining. One of those clammy evenings when you can't tell whether you're hot or chilled: hence the fire. But the doctor had finally allowed Beth to switch to crutches, and Beth had announced she was stir-crazy, so she and Sophie had invited themselves to the Potter's House for supper.

"I see Gran's been busy while I've been out of circulation," Beth said, nodding toward the row of damp-wrapped clay forms on the shelves.

"Are you surprised?" I shook my head, remembering. "Serena the indestructible. She's been over here nearly every morning, before I was awake. Great-Aunt Alexandra's situation must be tearing her up, but she's never breathed a word since it happened. Not to me, not to anybody."

"That's what you think," Sophie said. "If you mean has she broken down, no. Stiff upper lip and all that.

But she's been on the phone all day today, talking to Uncle Roger and Aunt Lisa, talking to her solicitor and to Great-Aunt Alexandra's solicitor overseas." *Solicitor* was the British word for lawyer. "She had me busy all afternoon, phoning hospitals, and nursing homes, and doctors, asking for information."

"It's handy for Gran, having a family member on the switchboard," Beth said with an odd edge on her voice. "No outsiders need know about the crack in the family image."

"That's not fair," Sophie said, somewhat to my surprise. "You don't want the poor old girl getting into the gossip papers, do you? They'd have a field day."

"I'm just glad I didn't get stuck making the calls," Beth said frankly.

"I don't mind. I kind of like it." Sophie looked self-consciously sheepish; then she laughed. "Tell you the truth, running that switchboard's really rather jolly. That's a laugh, isn't it? Me getting a bang out of Gran's business office! I rather like the business side of things, actually. I wouldn't mind going into it."

Beth and I did a double-take at Sophie the rebel reverting to British understatement. "You're kidding," Beth said at last.

"I'm not, actually." Sophie poured herself another cup of tar-black tea and dosed it liberally with milk and sugar. "I had a talk with Mummy on the phone last night," she said off-handedly. "Told her I'd decided to stay on here with Serena for the winter. Serena thinks I can be a jolly good help on the business side. Turns out I'm not half bad at figures on a computer. Serena wants to train me for it if I'll toe the line. Useful to have a family member keeping the family financial secrets, and all that. Don't look at me as if I've gone barmy, you two. It's a bloody good way to avoid that blasted Swiss finishing school!"

"Not to mention all the great guys you're apt to meet," Beth murmured slyly.

"Well, yes, there is that." Sophie patted her currently golden hair. But there was a wry look in her eyes. So Sophie, too, was discovering talents she hadn't known she had, I thought, amused.

The only person who wasn't getting anywhere this summer was Beth, and that was so unfair. Beth, the one person who'd found her talent and direction before any of us. "When did the doctor say you could start dancing again?" I asked Beth on Monday, the first day I'd gotten to talk to her alone.

"Not for six to eight weeks. He says I never should have tried to dance on that ankle after the first time I twisted it, not till it healed."

I refrained from pointing out that that was exactly what I'd told her.

"At least," Beth added savagely, "I'm free of Madame. She's leaving for California the first of September. Thank God!"

"You should have talked to Gran about her."

Beth just looked at me. "Don't you know yet what it's like to 'talk to Gran'? My gosh, after one week here I understood Aunt Kay a whole lot better!"

"I don't see the comparison," I said with dignity. "Mom's never tried to talk things out with Serena, as far as I can see. She just runs away! She talks a good line, but she always just runs away."

"You really don't understand, do you?" Beth sounded tired. "Gran's so strong. She's like that line of President Kennedy's that Mom and I saw inscribed at the Kennedy Memorial. Something about 'Others look at things as they are, and ask "Why?" I see things as they could be and I say, "Why not?" ' That's Gran. She has her visions of what could be—for all of us—and with the best will in the world she tries to make those things come true. The trouble is, she never asks us whether we want those things. She never asked your mother, did she? She never asked any of us what we wanted to do this summer."

"That's different," I said stubbornly. "I asked to stay here. Okay, I know you and Sophie didn't. But the things Gran made us do were right for us. All but Madame as your teacher, and how was Gran to know about that? You wouldn't tell her! My mother never gave Gran an even break. Any more than she did Dad and me."

"How much of a break have you given her?" Beth murmured beneath her breath, and then added, "Okay,

I'm not being fair. We'll leave Aunt Kay out of it and stick to you and me. Gran's been good for you because you've got backbone. You're not afraid to stand up to her when the chips are down."

"Don't tell me you're afraid of Gran!"

"Not of Gran. I'm just not strong like you two are," Beth said at last. "I just want peace, not confrontations. You wouldn't, not at *any* price. Look how you stood up to our dear family over those Living Pictures. You *made* them shape up. I can't do that. That's why somebody with convictions as strong as Gran's can run right over me. Like a hurricane."

"The only calm place in a hurricane is in its eye."

The words came from me involuntarily, in a whisper, and Beth looked at me, startled. "What?"

"Nothing. Just something somebody said to me." I turned to Beth impulsively. "Look, I didn't know I had any power till it bounced up out of nowhere when I needed it. When having those darn Living Pictures turn out right mattered to me. But Beth, I have seen you have Gran's kind of power. When you dance. I saw it when you didn't know I was watching, and it bowled me over. You do have the magic, and it will grow. You don't have to worry about whether you'll be strong enough or good enough."

Beth gave me a long look. "You really don't understand, do you? Never mind. At least I'm rid of Madame. And I didn't have to dance before Takalevsky."

Beth's words haunted me as the week went on. Beth

the perfectionist, who thought she wasn't good enough. Beth dreading having to dance inadequately before the master. Beth, who was actually sick at the prospect of letting Serena down.

It wasn't anything I could discuss with anyone, except my mother, and after the void between us I couldn't belt her with that over the telephone. I did, after a lot of thought, call Dad, but I couldn't find him in either Philadelphia or Wisconsin. The Philadelphia switchboard wanted to know if I wished to leave a message, and I said no thanks. No point in alarming Dad with paranoid suspicions.

So Beth wasn't dancing for the rest of the summer, and Sophie wasn't going back to the punk life in Europe. More changes. Another change that wasn't as visible or pin-down-able was between me and Carl. Something had been altered by that brief kiss, and we both knew it. Oh, we acted exactly the same toward each other, but I felt self-conscious.

The second week in August went by. Gran received charming thank-you letters for her hospitality from Takalevsky and ver Veyl, and three dozen roses. Beth received their notes of encouragement and autographed pictures. "Hang them on the wall," Sophie said, but Beth shook her head and put them away somewhere. "Too painful to look at, I suppose," Sophie said to me later, wisely.

"I wonder."

Liu showed up on Friday, back early from his vacation.

"Honolulu too hot, relatives too boring," he said flatly to Gran's scolding, and took command of her kitchen again. Gran had us all over for dinner Saturday night, and the cuisine was several classes higher than our own recent efforts. Great-Aunt Alexandra was there, but she just pushed her food around on her plate. She was miles away in some world of silence of her own.

There was a thunderstorm that night, sometime after midnight. The lightning woke me, and I crept around in the dark, shutting windows and admiring the lightning behind the willow trees. I could see Beth limping around next door on the same errand. She looked over, and waved, and I waved back. I was going to miss Beth when we left here. If we left here. Maybe I should think about staying. But even as the idea warmed me, I had the uneasy conviction that, close as Beth and I had become, there was some unknown territory inside her that she hadn't let me enter at all.

On Sunday morning the suffocating blanket of heat was gone. Vredezucht was like a toy village, scrubbed and shining and set out to dry in the faint breeze. Beth insisted on crossing the green to church on her new crutches, instead of going by car. The fragrance of Gran's biblical herb garden mixed with the scent of late summer roses rambling up the church.

Great-Aunt Alexandra wasn't there this morning,

but Gran was, kneeling in her familiar pew with her head bowed. Sophie and Beth and I slipped in beside her. The church bells chimed, and the organ pealed, and everything felt so safe and so familiar, like small-town summer Sundays back through childhood. There wasn't any regular choir during the summer. There were soloists, duets or trios, or groups: choir members who weren't on vacation, visitors passing through, sometimes one or more of Gran's VIPs. Today there was a group of kids from the local high school choir, and they sang a song that my youth group back home sang, too.

> To ev'ry thing . . .
> . . . Turn! Turn! Turn!
> There is a season . . .
> . . . Turn! Turn! Turn!
> And a time to ev'ry purpose
> under heaven . . .

The words seemed the sum and distillation of this summer. "Changes . . ."

The scripture reading was the Parable of the Talents, and the familiar words struck at me with new meaning.

> . . . the kingdom of heaven is like a man going into a far country, who called his servants together, and distributed to them his talents.

To one he gave five talents, and to another three, and to another one. . . . and when he returned he called his servants together for a reckoning. . . . the man who had been given five talents said, "Behold, I have made for you five talents more." . . . But the man who had received one talent said, "I was afraid, and hid my talent in the earth."

And the uninvested talent was taken away from him, and there was weeping and gnashing of teeth. Talents were like that, weren't they? If they were buried, undiscovered, unused, they atrophied just as the doctor was afraid Beth's leg might atrophy. I glanced over at Beth and saw that her eyes were bright with tears.

The sermon was about the Parable of the Talents, too. Sophie, on my other side, scribbled a note on her bulletin and passed it over to me. It said: "Can we be sure our Gran didn't write this?" Because the sermon was Gran's philosophy all over. Our gifts—whether intellect, or wealth, or talents—are ours in trust, to use for the greater good. Ignored, or used for ego trips, they disappeared or were distorted. Use it or lose it. The minister put it a lot more elegantly than that, just as Gran would. But it came down to the same thing—everything Vredezucht, everything Gran's life, stood for.

When the minister finished speaking there was a

brief silence before the organ swelled into the closing hymn. And in that silence there was a jarring sound, the sound of Beth's crutches, clattering as she pushed out of the pew. She limped down the aisle as fast as she could travel, and Sophie and I just sat there, dumbstruck. Then the organist came to, and everybody jumped up like corks popping out of bottles. I ran out after Beth, ignoring protocol.

I caught up with her as she was struggling down the steps. She pushed me off. "No! Just let me alone!" She started off doggedly across the green, and I didn't dare to follow.

Gran and Sophie caught up with me by now. "What's wrong with that girl?" Sophie demanded.

"I don't know. It's all tied up with her dancing, I do know that. She's afraid she's not good enough, or is not going to be able to, or something."

"You'd better go after her," Gran said, not moving.

"No. She doesn't want me. I'm no good to her right now," I said baldly, "and I don't know why."

"I'll go," Sophie said swiftly. She ran off.

Gran walked blindly across the road, into the biblical garden, and sat down on her boulder. I followed her.

"I'm no help for her," Gran said quietly, not turning. "Not for her, not for Alexandra anymore, not for Kay or Rena. I've done everything I could for them, and to them, and they're in some other world. We can't connect."

"Me neither," I said ungrammatically, sitting down, too. "If it's any help, Beth does know you're doing your best for her. I think in some corner of her pixilated mind, Mom knows that, too."

"All I want," Gran said, shaking her head, "is to make life less hard for them. To provide an environment in which their gifts could flourish. I know what it's like not to have that. I wanted to give it to others, especially the family. All wrapped up in tissue paper and silver bows."

Leave it to Gran to be able to reach for humor, even now. I reached over and hugged her. "Did it ever occur to you," I asked carefully, "that maybe your visions are too strong for us? That we wonder if we can live up to them?"

"You're not like that."

That's all you know, I thought inwardly. Aloud I said, "That's one of the things I've found out this summer. I do have Van Zandt strength. But not everybody has that much, or trusts enough. It's like you told me about how some of these herbs need rocky soil, and some rich loam, and some wet feet. And some need more shade than others. Gran, your light's awfully bright."

Gran looked at me, and a small smile played around her mouth. She laughed and kissed me. "Come on, let's go home before any of our curious neighbors come to find out what's wrong." She reached out a hand so I could help her up. It was the first time she'd ever done that. I was struck, suddenly, by how old and vulnerable Gran really was. Usually her charisma kept that from showing.

"Are you coming for Sunday dinner?" Gran asked. I shook my head.

"I think I'd better hang around the Potter's House, in case Beth decides to wander over." So I went home and disciplined myself to leave the first move to Beth, and Beth didn't make it.

In the middle of the afternoon the van drove up and Carl got out, carrying the Shaker rocker. "It turned out so well, your grandmother thought you might like to have it here. It goes with the other furnishings."

"Yes, I would." I led the way into the living room, and he followed. "Would you like some iced tea?"

"Thanks."

I sat in the rocker, and he sat on the stool by the potter's wheel, and we avoided looking at each other.

"This is ridiculous," Carl said at last. "Look, I heard about Beth. I suppose the whole town has. Small towns are like that. Everybody's brimming with well-wishes and concern, and that can get pretty sticky, can't it?"

"You said it."

"So how about getting out of town? We'll go out on the highway and get dinner somewhere. No strings. Get your mind off family."

"You don't have to take me out to cheer me up."

"I know I don't," Carl said cheerfully. "It's not even my main reason for inviting you, but it makes a darn good excuse."

"Okay," I said and took a deep breath. "I'd love to."

We went out to a quiet restaurant that Carl knew of and had pasta and veal parmigiana. It wasn't quite up to Liu's cooking, but it was familiar and comforting. There was a jukebox, and somebody was feeding it quarters for old standards. We danced, and that felt comfortable, too. When the music stopped, we sat down again and talked. I told Carl about church that morning, and Carl said he knew all about the Parable of the Talents. "My old man had another way of putting it. 'You durn well better use the brains the good Lord gave you!' I got pretty darn sick of hearing that when I was a kid, but he was right."

"What bothers me the most is that I've known all summer something's been bothering Beth, and I can't get to the bottom of it. Not by asking, not by goading, not by comforting. I've gotten to the point of doing nothing, and that's wrong."

"Not always," Carl said. "Have you had any physics classes, Laura? There's a difference between inert matter and nonmoving matter. Something can be still and yet be dynamic. Haven't you ever heard of active listening?"

"The calm in the hurricane's eye."

"You got it." Carl looked at his watch, then reached

for his wallet. "I think I'd better be getting you back home."

We drove back to Vredezucht. Carl parked in front of the Potter's House, came around and opened the door for me, and walked me up the steps. "Do you want to sit a while?" I asked.

"I don't think that would be a good idea." But he stood there, not moving. Then, as if neither of us could help ourselves, we moved into each other's arms. This was a real kiss, not like the one he'd given me before, and not at all like Jay's, but *real*.

When we drew apart, I was shaking, and Carl's face looked pale in the moonlight. "That was not," he said carefully, "a very good idea."

"Why not?" I whispered, just as carefully.

"You know." He managed a smile. "Robbing the cradle. Boss exploiting the employee. Or what's worse, employee coming on to the big boss's granddaughter."

"I'm not in the cradle. I thought we'd discussed that already," I said steadily. "And you know darn well nobody's exploiting anybody. Would you feel the same way if I weren't Laura Serena, and we were both five years older?"

"If we were five years older, you'd be twenty-one and I'd be out of grad school and there'd be no problem," Carl said ruefully. "Our timing's bad. But as your grandmother's fond of saying, 'Time moves in a spiral, and all things change.' " He touched me on the hand, gently, and then he left.

XVIII

 Journal—Sunday, August 7

. . . A time to rend, and a time to sew;
  a time to keep silence, and a time to speak;
A time to love, and a time to hate;
  a time of war, and a time of peace.

ECCLESIASTES 3:7–8

I went inside and to bed, but there were so many things on my mind I couldn't sleep. At least I thought I couldn't. I tossed and turned, and then all of a sudden I was staring at the window as the first glow of dawn showed behind the trees.

All my excess baggage was still lying around waiting for me, like a ring of gremlins. The biggest gremlin had Beth's name pinned to it.

"Enough, already," I told myself sternly and went

downstairs. I didn't want coffee. I got out some orange juice, and then I saw the potter's wheel. Gran had been here again, last night while I was out, and she'd been so not herself that she'd left her work sitting on the potter's wheel, uncovered. I took it off, wrapped it carefully in wet paper towels and plastic, and put it with her other pieces on the shelf. Then I stood, looking at the potter's wheel for quite a while.

Summer was nearly over, and I still hadn't learned to "center." Nobody'd said I had to; that was probably why not succeeding at it bothered me. Like a sleepwalker, I went to the clay bin and took some out, shaping it carefully into a sphere. Then I sat down at the potter's wheel.

I wasn't even really seeing the wheel. As a matter of fact, my eyes were full of tears. But I saw that center somewhere inside my head, behind my vision, and I just aimed the clay at it and started pedaling.

I wasn't thinking at all about what I was doing. I wasn't really thinking about anything. I was just feeling, the way I'd sometimes done when working on the Shaker rocker. Then I'd felt the grain of the wood, and the satin finish, and seen an image of the finished chair inside my head, and smelled the varnish. Now I felt the cool moistness of the clay and the steady turning. I could feel the rhythm of the pedal in my foot and all up through my body. I could smell the clay and the roses blooming with the dawn outside my window.

And a weird thing happened. I wasn't seeing a clay pot, real or idealized. I was seeing Beth dancing. Beth dancing when she thought she was alone. Beth dancing for an audience.

All at once the wheel wasn't moving anymore. I came out of my daze slowly, to find sunlight pouring through the windows, and the hands of the clock at eight, and a perfectly centered, urn-shaped vase sitting quietly between my hands on the potter's wheel. And I knew the answer to what was wrong with Beth.

Half in a trance, I rose and set the little vase beside Gran's work to dry. It was finished, complete; I had no need to do anything more to it. What I had was a need to go to Beth. I went upstairs, dressed, and went out to find her.

Somehow I knew where she'd be, even though it didn't make sense. Beside the river. She was there, dangling her bare feet in the water with her crutches laid carefully to one side. I scrambled down to sit beside her.

"It's dancing, isn't it?" I asked quietly. "You don't want to do it anymore."

Beth looked at me, startled, then away. She skipped a stone into the water and we listened to it splash. "I don't know *what* I want," she said at last. "But no, I don't want to dance."

"You idiot, why didn't you just tell somebody?"

"How could I?" Beth asked simply. "Mother's so

proud of me. Gran's so proud. All my life they've both been trying to pave the way—get me the right schools, the right teachers. Nothing else must waste Beth's time. I couldn't ever just be . . . ordinary."

"You're not ordinary. I don't think anybody is. That's beside the point. Why should you have to dance if you don't want to?"

"You know the answer to that," Beth said. "Didn't you listen to that blasted sermon? Haven't you had that line about your duty to use your talents hammered into you since you were a kid? Or wasn't Aunt Kay like that?"

"No, she wasn't. But I sure heard her rebellion against the line enough. My gosh, she's been living her rebellion right up till she got hooked on this latest project! I guess that's one of the differences between you and me," I said thoughtfully. "You always knew what your big talent was. I grew up not knowing I had talents."

"You do have them," Beth said.

"Uh-huh. That's one of the things I've learned this summer."

"That's another difference," Beth went on. "You've got lots of talents. And you're strong. You fight for what matters to you. I can't do that. All I can do is dance. That's what's been driving me crazy. Do I have to dance, just because I can? Gran and her darn 'talents are a blessing!' " she said bitterly. "If you ask me they're more like millstones around our necks."

I told Beth about my conversation with Dad, and what he'd said about being able to recognize our real calling by the joy-in-doing.

"That's the way dance used to be," Beth said. "It still is, sometimes, when I'm all alone. But I don't want audiences! Not now, not ever. I don't want that life."

"So don't have it."

"Suppose that's the only gift I have?"

"Oh, for Pete's sake," I said with vigor, "you're fourteen years old. You're a Van Zandt! And do you honestly think there's anyone on the face of this earth who's ever been any good at just one thing?"

Beth started to giggle. She laughed and laughed, and we rolled on the riverbank till we fell in. Then, seeing as we were thoroughly messed up, we swam a little. We sat on the bank till the sun dried us. Then we walked home, and there weren't any barriers between us anymore.

"There's just one problem . . . two problems," Beth said when we reached Wisteria Cottage.

"Gran and Aunt Lisa. Don't worry about them. As you pointed out, confrontations on things that matter to me are *my* talent." I gave her a hug and a little push, and then I went back to the Potter's House to clean up for the most important diplomatic mission of my life.

I didn't go to work that day. I went to Gran's. I found her on her screened porch, sipping coffee. "Gran,"

I said, "we've got to talk. I think you'd better pour me some of that coffee, too."

"But why didn't the poor child tell me?" Gran asked, bewildered, when I was done. A shadow passed over her face. "Is she—are the rest of you—really that afraid of me?"

"Face it, Gran, like I told you before, you come on strong!" I said it with a smile, and then I went and kissed her. "I don't think it's so much that people are afraid of you; they're afraid of letting you down. Your visions matter so much to you, you draw people into them with you. Sometimes they . . . lose sight of their own visions. They get . . . cannibalized."

Gran winced.

"I didn't mean that the way it sounded," I said hastily.

"No, you're right. I do see possibilities in people so intensely that when they're less intense, it seems to me like there's no fire in them at all. So," Gran said ruefully, "I try to light their fires. I've always been good at that."

"Maybe too darn good."

Gran nodded. "Meaning there's room for candles in the world as well as beacon fires? Point taken. I'll try to learn to give people—what is it your mother's always talking about? Give them space." She rose. "Thank you, Laura. Go tell Beth she can stop worrying. You stop worrying, too. I'll have the talk with Lisa for you."

Gran stood looking at me for a minute, her hands

resting lightly on my shoulders, a tender half smile on her face. Then she kissed my forehead, gave me a little pat, and sent me on my way.

"Oh, by the way," I called back casually from the doorway, "I've finally got the hang of the potter's wheel. I thought you'd like to know."

XIX

Journal—August 21

Our revels now are ended.

—SHAKESPEARE *The Tempest*

All things must change
To something new, to something strange . . .

—HENRY WADSWORTH LONGFELLOW

Winds of change. Dad came for a quick visit, from late one afternoon to early the following morning, en route once again from Wisconsin to Philadelphia. He walked into the workshop and surprised me. I introduced him to Carl, and they hit it off at once, as I knew they would.

"Knock off early and take your father for a tour of our latest installation," Carl said.

As we toured the exhibit, I realized with a little start that now Dad and I shared a second language, not just a family one. The language of shared work. There wasn't so much difference between what Dad did and what I'd been doing. We now had a lot of interests and enthusiasms in common.

When we finished the tour, Dad looked at his watch. "I promised Serena I'd be with her at five-thirty. I'm taking you both to the Monongahela House for dinner. Why don't you take my bag back to the Potter's House, and get changed and meet us there at six-thirty?"

So Dad had already been in touch with Gran. They were probably going to talk about me. The thought didn't bother me. I could, as Beth said, hold my own.

I went home, paid Beth's shower a quick visit, and put on my chiffon dress. Then I walked through the late August sunlight over to the hotel. Waves of scent, the sweetness of stock and the spiciness of thyme and the tang of lemon balm, came from Gran's gardens.

Gran and Dad were already seated at a window table in the dining room, and they had indeed been discussing me. They straightened as I approached, Gran with her vague radiant smile and Dad with a twinkle for me in his eye. I sat down demurely and waited to see who would drop the shoe.

It was Gran, of course—I should have known from that twinkle—and she waited till the waiter had served us seafood cocktails and withdrawn. Gran speared a piece of crabmeat, looked at it with mild interest, and then at me.

"Your father tells me he is going to be back in Elm Grove through the end of September. But his schedule after that is uncertain. We've been discussing options. A housekeeper, of course. One place or the other. Or you can stay here. There's a fine school, and with things still unsettled about Alexandra, I plan to stay here myself at least through Christmas. I'd love to have you, and your father's willing. We both agree that being here this summer has been good for you."

"I know it has." I reached a hand across the table to my father, and he took it. I took a breath. "Thank you, Gran, for everything. I'm going to stay with Dad—wherever he is." I took another breath and smiled. "I can take a rain check for visiting here a lot, can't I?"

Gran's eyes were luminous. "The Potter's House is yours, yours and your dad's, whenever you want it. I won't use it for any other guests. You may want to leave some clothes there, so you'll have them handy."

I appreciated the way she worded that, as a suggestion, not an instruction or command. "I'd like that," I said. "So long as you'll still use the place when you want to. For guests or the potter's wheel."

"I'm going back to Elm Grove the day after tomorrow," Dad said, when we were back on the Potter's House porch. "You want to come with me, or stay here through Labor Day?"

"I'll come. I'd kind of like to plug into the crowd again there before school starts."

I felt another little start of recognition as I said that. I did have friends back there, even a couple of guys who kind of liked me. I hadn't been thinking about them at all, not since I'd come here into a circle of relatives who'd been almost strangers.

Correction: I hadn't been thinking about them since I'd got caught up in the whirlwind, not just of Serena, but of Mom and Dad's dissolving marriage. That didn't seem like such a whirlwind anymore. I'm not saying I was thrilled about the situation, and I still hadn't talked to Mom, but at least thinking about all that no longer gave me the shakes. I was no longer braced against catastrophe.

And Gran and Beth and Sophie—yes, even Jay, too, in his way—were no longer unknown quantities, no longer just relatives. They were friends. Closer friends than any I'd ever known. The fact that we were blood kin, too, was the icing on the cake.

And then there was Carl. Carl. After I said good-bye to Dad at seven the next morning, I went to the workshop through the early morning sunlight. Carl was already there, whistling as he laid out his tools—plane and awl and level, metal brushes and varnish, and the delicate equipment for gold leafing. I was going to miss working with those things, miss the smell of the varnish and the leather cases, and Carl's skilled sensitive hands.

"I hear you're pulling out tomorrow afternoon," Carl said, smiling. "It won't be the same around here in another week. Half the apprentices have early college openings. I'm leaving next Friday myself. I want to spend Labor Day weekend with my folks." And then, "Hey, no need to turn on the water faucets! It's not the end of the world, you know. Serena's offered me this job again next summer. She even wants me to come in as a consultant during my winter break. And you do know, don't you, that you have a job waiting here any time you want it. I say so, and Serena says so, too. Laura, if you must cry, please don't do it over that chest. The varnish isn't dry."

I moved hastily and wiped my eyes on a paint rag. "Sorry, I know I'm being silly."

"No, you're not. You're just not looking at the big picture," Carl said. "Hand me a rag, will you? And the turpentine." He started repairing the damage that I'd caused. "What I'm trying to say is, things aren't ending. They're just changing."

"There've been too darn many changes," I said ruefully. "I could do with something to hold on to. And there isn't anything."

"Oh, yes, there is," Carl contradicted. "There's what's in you. There's what you told me about the potter's wheel. If you keep focused on the vision of what-can-be, the wheel turns but the center remains constant."

The peace in the eye of the hurricane, again.

"You're not the only one who has a grandmother

that likes to hand out platitudes," Carl added. "Mine's Norwegian. She came here as an immigrant, all by herself, as a teenage girl. Another of your survivor types."

"It does seem to run in the genes, doesn't it," I murmured wickedly.

Carl laughed. "True! So do the black Norwegian moods, which fortunately I've managed to avoid. Anyway, my grandmother says the earth turns, and we'd durn well better turn with it, because if we try to stand in one place we end up going backwards. She's not strong on science, but she sure does know about life. So you're leaving tomorrow. How would you feel about dinner somewhere tonight?"

"I'd feel fine," I answered firmly.

I had an idea Gran would be expecting me to eat with her, but I'd done that last night. So in order to avoid the embarrassment of turning down an invitation, I got hold of Sophie at the switchboard and asked her to let Gran know my plans.

"Good for you," Sophie said enthusiastically. "I hear you're going home with Uncle Ken. Come to my digs and fill me in, okay?"

So Sophie and Beth and I had lunch for the last time in Sophie's place. It really was Sophie's place, now.

She'd started tacking rock-concert posters on the wall. "With Gran's permission, would you believe? I do think she's pleased I decided to stay on."

"Of course she's pleased, you idiot," Beth laughed.

She was laughing a lot lately. Getting the ballet millstone off her neck had turned her into a new person. She was even, I noted with satisfaction, gaining weight.

"So what are you going to do?" Sophie asked her, after we'd thoroughly reviewed my plans, such as they were so far.

"Mom's coming back here over Labor Day," Beth said. "She and Uncle Roger are flying together. There's going to be a conference about Great-Aunt Alexandra. Then I'm going back to London with Mom. She's looking into schools there. I've never had time to concentrate on anything but dance before, but I think I'd like to study languages. And art."

So none of us branches were falling too far from the family tree. And what a tree—I pictured Gran painted, surrealistically, as a primordial tree, and giggled. The others wanted to know why, and I told them, and when we finished wiping our eyes, Beth said she'd pass the suggestion on to Aunt Lisa. *Portrait of Serena as a Tree*—with a caftan on the trunk, and a silver cross, and all of us with our various gifts as branches."

"And diamonds," Sophie added, "definitely diamonds."

"No, that should be Great-Aunt Alexandra. A tall thin Christmas tree, draped with lace and Serena the Third's necklace and a tiara." For a minute two pictures of Great-Aunt Alexandra, as she'd been the first night, and then at the benefit, came to me sharply, and I stopped laughing.

"And Jay as an automobile," Sophie said quickly. "Definitely an automobile— with the brakes not working!" We went on inventing surrealistic portraits of our various relations, and I got back to work quite late.

Carl picked me up at six-thirty, and to my surprise he headed out of the village. "I thought we both needed to get away from the museum village atmosphere," he said. "The air here is dynamic, but it starts to seem stale if you stay in it too long. Museums are for refueling in, not living in." We drove to Pittsburgh and took a dinner cruise on a riverboat from Station Square. Sunset gilded the windows of the skyscrapers in the Golden Triangle; a band played and a calliope tooted. Later there was moonlight and dancing. We didn't talk about the summer. We talked about what we'd be doing through the winter.

"We'll be in Philadelphia at least half the time, Dad says. Remember what I said about coming for a tour of Dad's project."

"I remember," Carl said. "You remember what I said about museum management courses."

We drove back to Vredezucht, barely touching, but very conscious of each other's nearness. Carl walked me up the steps of the Potter's House and then paused.

"I don't know how good an idea this is," he said, "but I guess I should listen to some of my own sermons about taking risks." And he bent and kissed me. He didn't hold me; we were scarcely touching, but he kissed me. Not a long kiss, but a real one, with a promise of future years to come. Then, without our exchanging another word, he went down the steps and I went inside. It wasn't good-bye; it wasn't an ending; it was simply change.

I didn't go to the workshop the next morning. I washed my car, which Gran had agreed to garage for me to use on my visits to Vredezucht. I finished packing, and I cleaned the Potter's House from top to bottom. I left half my summer clothes in the closet for next year. Or for weekends in early fall, perhaps, if warm weather held. Beth came over to help me, and at lunchtime Sophie arrived with hero sandwiches. We picnicked together on the porch.

"So, did you bid farewell to the Viking god?" Sophie asked. I blushed. "I'll say she did," Beth murmured innocently. "I just happened to be at a window."

"Don't knock it till you've tried it," I said wickedly. Now it was Beth who reddened.

"I meant to ask you. Any message for Aunt Kay when I see her in London?" she asked.

"Don't start that. Either of you. I'm going to write her, as soon as I get back home. I will, really."

I knew I had to do that, but I really wasn't thinking about Mother at the moment. I was thinking about that word *home*. When Mother took off, I'd felt as if I no longer had one. That wasn't true. Not in the literal sense. It wasn't that I didn't *have* one; I didn't have *one*. Not just one. Home, I thought with satisfaction, was inside me. Home was wherever my heart was, wherever I had friends and kin. I had many homes. I was rich indeed.

"Got to get back to the old switchboard," Sophie said, scrambling up. "See you soon." She kissed me and departed. Beth stayed till we saw the surrey coming around the corner of the green, with Gran at the reins. Then Beth kissed me and hugged me hard. "Thanks for everything. I really love you. Please write." She pulled away, eyes bright with tears, and limped back to Wisteria Cottage as fast as her leg would let her.

Gran's eyes, too, were wet. But her smile was radiant. "My dear, I'm feeling sorry for myself over losing you. But I really do believe you've made the right decision."

I hugged her. "You're not losing me. You can't ever lose me."

"Before you go," Gran said, "I have some new sketches for the conference center I'd like to go over with you." So we sat together on the porch swing, going over future plans, until Dad's rented car drew up.

"Ready to leave?" he asked, smiling.

"As soon as I get my suitcase." I went inside for it while Dad and Gran greeted each other by the surrey.

I took a last look around the quiet rooms. Everything was in order. My little vase had finally dried enough for firing. I tied a tag around its neck, *For Gran,* and parked it on the potter's wheel. It wasn't the world's greatest vase, not by a long shot, but Gran would understand. Then I picked up my carry-on bag and my suitcase, and went down the front steps. Dad came to take them.

"Got everything?" he asked. "No unfinished business? We have time to spare, if you need it."

"I'm ready to go. Everything's taken care of," I said. And then I paused. "No. Wait. I do have one more thing I want to do. You wait here, will you?"

I went inside, shutting the door behind me. Then I fumbled in my purse for my address book, picked up the phone, and punched a lot of numbers. My heart pounded as the phone gave off unfamiliar bleeps. Then, as near as if it were around the next corner, I heard the sound of a receiver being lifted, and a voice say, "Hello?"

I wet my lips. "Hello?" I said breathlessly. And then, after I had swallowed hard, "Hello, Mom, is that you? It's me, Laura. . . ."